"I'm relieved she's feeling so much better."

Arleta stretched to try to reach a bowl from the cupboard.

"Here, I'll get that for you," Noah offered. She stepped aside so he could retrieve the dish. Even so, as he pulled down a bowl, he was acutely aware that he hadn't stood this close to a single woman since he'd courted Hannah Miller.

Then it dawned on him: *Groossmammi* wasn't really that ill! She wanted Arleta and him to eat together without her. She was giving them privacy so they could get to know each other better. And that was why she'd retreated into the living room now, too. Or was it? Not that it mattered. Even if his grandmother was scheming to match him and Arleta, Noah wasn't going to develop a romantic relationship with her or with anyone else.

But that didn't mean Noah didn't notice what a sweet gap-toothed smile she gave him when he handed her the bowl.

Carrie Lighte lives in Massachusetts next door to a Mennonite farming family, and she frequently spots deer, foxes, fisher cats, coyotes and turkeys in her backyard. Having enjoyed traveling to several Amish communities in the eastern United States, she looks forward to visiting settlements in the western states and in Canada. When she's not reading, writing or researching, Carrie likes to hike, kayak, bake and play word games.

Visit the Author Profile page at Harlequin.com.

Hiding Her
Amish Secret

Carrie Lighte

LOVE INSPIRED
INSPIRATIONAL ROMANCE

LOVE INSPIRED®
INSPIRATIONAL ROMANCE

*Recycling programs
for this product may
not exist in your area.*

ISBN-13: 978-1-335-48883-1

Hiding Her Amish Secret

This edition published by arrangement with Harlequin Books S.A.

For questions and comments about the quality of this book,
please contact us at CustomerService@Harlequin.com.

Love Inspired
22 Adelaide St. West, 40th Floor
Toronto, Ontario M5H 4E3, Canada
www.Harlequin.com

Printed in U.S.A.

If we confess our sins, he is faithful and just
to forgive us our sins, and to cleanse us
from all unrighteousness.
—*1 John* 1:9

In memory of my great-uncle

Chapter One

Amish women typically owned four dresses: one for wash, one for wear, one for dress and one for spare. Anything more than that was considered excessive. But there was no limit on the number of socks they customarily owned, and Arleta Bontrager's filled half of her suitcase.

"I didn't know you had so many pairs," Leanna marveled as she sat on the bed, watching Arleta pack. "Do you really need to take them all?"

"*Jah*. You know how cold my feet always are," Arleta answered, feeling guilty for misleading her fourteen-year-old sister. But she would have felt worse for setting a poor example for her. Besides, her feet *were* often cold—although that's not why she wore socks every day. Actually, the reverse was truer; *because* she wore socks every day, her feet felt cold whenever she went without them.

"I'd hate it if my feet got too cold to go barefoot," Leanna said, holding her legs straight out in front of her and stretching her toes apart. "I love to feel the dew on the grass in the mornings when I'm hanging laundry and the softness of the earth in the garden."

"How about the stones or the heat of the pavement when you're walking down the road to your friend Emma's *haus*? Do you love that, too?" Arleta teased.

Leanna shrugged. "I walk on the shoulder of the road most of the way. When it comes time to cross the pavement, I run so quickly I hardly feel the heat."

Few of the women in their little community of Serenity Ridge, Maine, donned footwear during the warmer months, unless they were going to church or to one of the *Englisch* shops. Going barefoot was cooler, more convenient, and it saved wear and tear on their shoes. And as Leanna pointed out, going barefoot allowed them to appreciate the Lord's creation in a way they couldn't if they were wearing shoes all the time.

Arleta used to love it when the weather warmed enough for her to shed her shoes for the season, too. Not anymore. Now she rarely went without shoes and socks—or sandals and socks—outdoors. And when she was indoors, if she had to remove her shoes she always kept her socks on. She even wore them to bed. She'd gotten so used to wearing them they almost felt like a second skin.

"Maybe you have a low thyroid. Emma's *mamm* has that and it makes her fingers and toes cold," Leanna suggested.

"My fingers aren't cold. Feel." Arleta squeezed Leanna's hand. She didn't want her sister to repeat her comment about her thyroid in front of their mother, especially since Arleta was about to leave town for the next four months. She'd stop Arleta from going until she visited the doctor. And Arleta knew there was nothing wrong with her thyroid.

There wasn't even anything wrong with her feet. Nothing physically wrong, anyway. But beneath her socks, Arleta was hiding a shameful secret: two years ago she'd gotten a tattoo on her left ankle. The red heart with her *Englisch* boyfriend's initials in black ink was tiny, no bigger than her thumbnail. But it was in complete violation with Amish beliefs about modest appearances, especially for a female.

When she'd gotten it, Arleta was on her *rumspringa* and she had already decided she was leaving the Amish. In fact, that was exactly why she'd gotten the tattoo— to prove she intended to "go *Englisch*" and marry Ian Fairfax, the grandson of the people whose lake house she cleaned. She'd met Ian when he'd come to visit his grandparents in between his junior and senior years of college. His parents were going through a contentious divorce and Ian didn't want to stay with either of them, so he spent his summer at the lake house.

Ironically, Arleta was so levelheaded her parents hadn't had any qualms about her "working out," meaning working outside their community, with *Englisch-ers*. And Arleta certainly never intended to engage in a personal relationship with one. But Ian was utterly forlorn, and when he followed her around the house, practically begging her for conversation, she figured there was no harm in chatting with him…

And there wouldn't have been, if all they'd done was talked. But one thing led to another and by the end of the summer, she and Ian were so smitten with each other he asked her to marry him and she agreed. Since she had turned eighteen in August, they could have gotten married right then, but Arleta's father had suffered a heart attack that spring—that's why she had to work in the first place—and she wanted to wait until he was fully recovered before she broke the news to him that she was leaving the Amish. She suggested that Ian finish college first, and they could get married after he graduated.

Ian was crushed Arleta wanted to put off their wedding, which was understandable. After all, he'd just seen his parents break up after twenty-five years of marriage; Arleta had only known him less than four months. So she'd gotten the tattoo to show him there was no going back on her word. It was a symbol of her love for him. Of her intention to have him in her life forever.

But now it had become a symbol of her stupidity. Of how she'd almost given up everything she'd held dear. Her faith. Her family. Her community. And for what? A young man who told her—in a letter, no less—that he decided he was too young to get married. That he'd confused his feelings of dejection over his parents' divorce with love for Arleta. And that he hoped she'd find a good Amish man who would marry her and give her a family like she wanted.

Ha! What gut *Amish man would want to marry a woman with a tattoo of an* Englischer's *initials on her skin?* Arleta thought as she rolled another pair of socks to stuff into her suitcase.

She didn't know of any Amish boys who'd gotten a tattoo during *rumspringa*, much less girls. Girls were less likely to rebel against their customs during their *rumspringa* than boys were. Oh, they might wear their hair down and experiment with makeup, but they wouldn't do something that left a permanent mark, like getting their ears pierced. Or a tattoo. The most scandalous thing any girl in her district had done during *rumspringa* was to put purple streaks in her hair, but they washed out eventually.

Ideally, the Amish weren't supposed to hold what Arleta had done during her *rumspringa* against her now. The running around period was a time to test one's beliefs. To make sure the young person wanted to commit to the Amish faith and lifestyle. It was only after formalizing that commitment by being baptized into the church that the Amish were held accountable to the *Ordnung* as adults.

But in practice, Arleta knew that people would judge her if they found out she had a tattoo. She wouldn't have blamed them; she judged herself, too. Not just because of the tattoo, but because she'd pledged her love to an *Englischer*, which was a violation of her Amish faith, regardless of whether she'd been on *rumspringa* or not.

As much as she regretted the past, she couldn't undo it. She had confessed her sin to God and she'd repented and joined the Amish church, yet she couldn't seem to put her shame behind her. But maybe, just maybe she could get rid of the visual reminder of what she'd done. She'd heard that the *Englisch* had a procedure for erasing tattoos. It was expensive, but with what she earned from her new job—

Leanna's laughter interrupted Arleta's thoughts. "It

looks like you're bringing a pair for every day of the month, not for every day of the week."

"I don't want to run out of clean pairs."

"Your socks shouldn't get *that* dirty. It's not as if you're going to work on a potato farm."

"*Jah*, that's true. I'll probably spend most of my time indoors tending to Noah's *groossmammi*'s needs and cleaning and cooking. But I'm sure there's gardening to be done, too. I want to be prepared so I can help Noah however he needs me to help him."

Noah Lehman was a metal roofing installer who lived in New Hope, a tiny Amish community north of Serenity Ridge and Unity. Arleta had only spoken to him briefly on the phone, but she knew that his immediate family had all been killed in a house fire about six years ago. Noah hadn't told her that—she knew because all the *leit* from Serenity Ridge and Unity had helped rebuild the house. Usually barn raisings and house building were joyous occasions, but that one was so solemn it brought tears to Arleta's eyes just to remember it.

Now his groossmammi *is ill, what a pity*, she thought, snapping her suitcase closed.

Ordinarily, Amish families and communities pitched in to tend to those within their church districts who were ill, but the New Hope community was only about ten years old, and it was still so small that there weren't enough people to care for Noah's grandmother. So he had asked the deacons in Serenity Ridge and Unity to put the word out he was hiring a woman for the summer to take care of his grandmother, who had been undergoing cancer treatments and was recovering at home.

"I can't believe you're going all the way to New Hope," Leanna said with a sigh. "Now *Mamm* and I will really be outnumbered by the *buwe*. Are you sure you want to go?"

Although New Hope was only twenty miles away, it was a two-day round trip by buggy, and Arleta understood why her sister was confused by her decision. With the exception of the time when Arleta's father had a heart attack, she'd never worked outside of her home. Her role was to help her mother and Leanna with domestic chores, while Arleta's father and brothers supported the family financially, by working with an *Englisch* lumber company. But Noah's sad situation gave Arleta a worthwhile way to earn the income she required to have her tattoo removed and her family didn't object to her leaving, because they recognized Noah needed her assistance more than their own household did.

Knowing her little sister looked up to her and would be lonely without her around every day, Arleta assured Leanna. "*Jah*, I'm sure I want to go. I'll miss you, but it's only for a few months. May is almost over and I'll be back before September."

"What if you like New Hope so much you decide to stay there?"

"Don't be *lappich*. My *familye* is here," Arleta said. "My favorite little *schweschder* is here."

"But you might find a suitor there and fall in love and then he'll ask you to get married and stay in New Hope with him."

There's absolutely no chance of that happening. Arleta cupped her sister's chin and looked into her eyes. "I'll be back before you know it. And by then, you'll be so used to having an entire bedroom to yourself, you'll want me to leave again."

Leanna was still skeptical. "You promise you won't marry a potato *bauer* from New Hope?"

Arleta chuckled at her sister's fear that she'd meet and marry a potato farmer, as opposed to a man who had a different vocation. "I promise you, I'm not marrying a *bauer* of any kind." *I'm not marrying anyone, period.*

Noah Lehman stopped pacing in the living room to peer out the window. It was already eight forty-five. What was keeping Arleta Bontrager? He'd specifically asked that she arrange for the van to drop her off before eight o'clock in the morning so he could talk to her alone before his grandmother woke at eight thirty. She was already up, and Noah's *Englisch* coworker was due to pick him up at nine o'clock to take him to the house where they were finishing an installation.

For the past six years, Noah had been working for an Amish family's metal roofing supply and installation business. The owners, Colin and Albert Blank, were brothers who lived in Serenity Ridge. Because of Maine's harsh winters, metal roofs were in high demand and the Blank brothers had such a good reputation for their work that they began getting installation requests from *Englischers* who lived in New Hope, too. Initially, they'd turned down those orders, because the distance would have required them to travel too far and they didn't have enough employees to meet the demand. Although they did employ *Englischers* who transported equipment and metal sheeting to their various work-sites, the Blanks preferred the majority of their staff to be Amish.

That's where Noah and two other New Hope district members—David Hilty, a man in his late fifties, and Jacob Auer, a teenager—came in. Together, the men worked with Mike Hall, an *Englischer*. Mike drove a truck with supplies, and sometimes he picked up the other crew members when the site couldn't easily be reached by buggy. Maine had endured a particularly se-vere winter, so business was booming; no one wanted to be caught without a metal roof next year. Their four-man team was usually hard at work by seven or eight o'clock, but today Noah had asked them to postpone their start time so he could be home when Arleta ar-rived.

"You're going to make sawdust out of the floor-boards, pacing like that," his grandmother, Sovilla, scolded, but her tone was one of concern, not annoy-ance. "Arleta will get here when she gets here."

Her voice startled Noah and he glanced over at her. Instead of wearing her usual white organdy prayer *kapp* pinned to her hair, she had covered her bald scalp with a white kerchief. His grandmother used to have such dark hair and eyebrows—but even those had fallen out after the chemo treatments, along with her eyelashes. She looked so pale. So faded.

"*Jah.* But I hope she gets here before Mike does so I can let her in."

"I'm not so old I can't get off the sofa to answer the door."

Neh, but you might be too frail, Noah thought ruefully. *And she won't just* kumme *in, like our neighbors do.*

For the past two months, whenever Sovilla wasn't in the hospital, the deacon's wife, Almeda Stoll, and their nearest neighbor, Sarah Troyer, had been looking after her while Noah was at work. In exchange, Noah helped their husbands install metal roofing on their workshops and homes. But recently, Almeda had traveled out of state to help her ailing elderly sister. Sarah had just given birth to her first child, a son, so she could no longer tend to Sovilla, either.

Almost all of the other Amish women in New Hope, old and young alike, either had family or farming commitments that prevented them from staying with Noah's grandmother, too. Oh, they were more than willing to patch together a schedule that would allow for someone to drop in on her several times a day, but the more people who came in and out of the house, the greater her chances of catching an illness. Besides, Noah believed his grandmother needed someone with her around the clock as she recovered from her final round of cancer treatments.

That meant Noah either had to take time off from work for a couple of months until she was stronger and Sarah could return, or he had to hire someone from Serenity Ridge or Unity. While Noah wasn't particularly fond of the idea of a stranger, even an Amish one, living in their home with them, he knew a woman could take far better care of his grandmother and the house-keeping than he could. Plus, this was one of the busiest periods of installation. Even with Arleta's salary to pay, he'd still be making much more than what he'd lose if he took time off work.

Earning as much money now as he could was crucial, in preparation for providing his grandmother further medical care if her most recent course of treatment didn't work. Although the Amish community helped pay each other's major medical bills, Noah was reluctant to tap into New Hope's dwindling mutual aid fund more than he already had. Like most Amish, he'd been conscientious about what kind of medical services he'd agreed to for his grandmother, since American hospitals had a tendency to run all sorts of tests, which were costly and sometimes seemed unnecessary.

It wasn't unusual for the Amish to seek experimental treatments in Mexico, where medicine was less expensive. Still, there would be train tickets to buy and lodging expenses to pay. Not to mention, the loss of income while Noah was away. But he figured if his crew accepted every project they could between now and the time his grandmother had her next tests in a little over three months, and if he took on a few individual installations after hours himself...

"Did you hear me?" his grandmother asked, pulling him back to the present moment. "You seem a hundred miles away."

More like three thousand miles away, Noah thought, considering the distance between Maine and Mexico. But he didn't want to tell her about his plan because it might discourage her if she knew he was worried the treatment might not work. Worse, she'd reject the trip out of hand, saying it wasn't worth the expense. Better to earn the money first, and wait to see what the doctor said at her next appointment. "Sorry, I guess I was lost in thought."

"Aha," she uttered, and the familiar sparkle momentarily lit her dark brown eyes. "You're wondering what kind of *weibsmensch* Arleta will be and whether or not she already has a suitor, weren't you?"

"Neh!" he protested truthfully. "That's the furthest thing from my mind, *Groossmammi.*"

"Well, it shouldn't be. It's only natural for you to want to court. To get married and start a *familye* of your own."

Noah had heard this all before. Many, many times. He'd given up telling his grandmother he had no desire to court or get married. As for starting a family of his own, Noah just wished he had his old family back... He shuddered, thinking of his parents, two younger brothers and sister who died in a house fire one evening six years ago. Noah would have died, too, but he'd been out late. Too late.

Too late to make his curfew and too late to save his family from the fire he saw raging in the second story of the house when he pulled up the lane in his courting buggy. Even now, Noah had no recollection of getting out of the carriage and running into the house. All that stuck in his mind was the terrible noise of the roaring fire and the popping windowpanes. And the wall of heat that was as impenetrable as a wall of stone, stealing the breath from his lungs and prohibiting him from taking another step up the stairs.

And so he'd turned and run. Because his horse had gotten spooked and taken off with the buggy in tow, Noah had sprinted all the way to the phone shanty to call the *Englischers* for help.

"There was nothing you could have done to save them," the firefighters told him afterward. Even with their equipment and protective gear, they hadn't been able to rescue his family.

"It was *Gott*'s will," was the refrain he heard countless times from the deacon, his grandmother, and his Amish friends and community.

Noah tried hard to accept that, but deep down, he knew he was to blame. If he had returned home even fifteen minutes earlier, as he was supposed to—instead of lingering to kiss Hannah Miller on her porch swing— he *might* have been able to save his family.

Now, with the exception of a few cousins and an aunt in Michigan, his grandmother was the only family he had left and Noah was going to do everything humanly possible to preserve *her* life. God willing, the last treatments she'd had were effective—they'd find out in another ten weeks or so—but if they weren't, he wanted to be prepared. Which meant his sole focus was on praying for her healing and earning money for further treatment.

"Please don't start on me about courting, *Groossmammi*," he said affectionately. "You know how I feel—"

"I hear a vehicle. Is that her or is it Mike?" Sovilla interrupted, pointing to the window.

Noah turned to face the window again. A silver passenger van was driving up the dirt lane. "It's her."

"Well, don't just stand there. Go carry her suitcase in for her. Make her feel *wilkom*," his grandmother instructed, sitting up straight and adjusting her kerchief.

Noah shoved his feet into his boots at the door and trotted outside and down the porch steps just as the van was pulling away.

"Hi, Arleta. I'm Noah," he said as the short woman with strawberry-blond hair approached him. "I can take that for you."

Young, full-figured and energetic, Arleta looked perfectly capable of carrying her own suitcase, but she extended it to him anyway. "*Denki*. I'm sorry I'm late. The driver was following GPS and it directed him to the pond on the other side of Pleasant Road. It's a *gut* thing I still remembered where your *haus* was from when I came here for the—"

Arleta stopped walking and cupped her hand over her mouth, obviously embarrassed. Noah realized she must have come there when the nearby Amish communities helped build a new house. As painful as it was for him to acknowledge the past, he was relieved that Arleta apparently already knew what happened to his family. It meant there'd be no troublesome questions later. "For the *haus* building?"

"*Jah*." Her light green eyes, fringed with pale lashes, were full of remorse. "I'm so sorry."

He didn't know whether she meant she was sorry

for bringing it up or sorry about what happened to his family. Either way, that was as far as he wanted the conversation to go, so he gave a brusque nod of acknowledgment and then said, "Let's go inside. I want to introduce you to my *groossmammi* before my coworker arrives to pick me up."

To his surprise, instead of resting on the sofa, his grandmother was putting a coffeepot on the stove. "I'm Sovilla. *Wilkom* to our *haus*, Arleta."

"*Denki.* I'm very glad to be here."

Seeing Arleta wiping her shoes on the round braided rug at the door, Noah interjected, "Since my *groossmammi*'s immune system is compromised, you'll need to remove your shoes at the door so you don't track in germs."

"Oops, I'm sorry." Three wrinkles etched her forehead when she asked, "Is it all right if I leave my socks on? My...my feet get cold."

Noah hesitated. "I suppose that's okay, as long as they're clean."

Arleta's cheeks pinkened. "*Jah*, they're clean."

"Of course she's wearing clean socks," Noah's grandmother asserted, giving him a little scowl. To Arleta, she said, "I'm always cold, too, Arleta. You and I are going to get along like two peas in a pod."

As Arleta bent over to unlace her shoes, Sovilla shook her head at Noah, no doubt to express her disapproval for embarrassing Arleta when she'd just barely crossed their threshold. Noah didn't care. His grandmother's health was at stake. Her *life* was at stake. He'd say or do whatever he needed in order to protect her.

Besides, he asked everyone to remove their shoes at the door, so why should Arleta be any different?

"I'm afraid I need to go sit back down in the other room," Sovilla said apologetically. "Noah, why don't you take Arleta's suitcase to her room for her? She can pour us a cup of *kaffi*."

Stepping out of his boots, Noah dutifully carried Arleta's suitcase down the hall. Noah had cleared his belongings out of his room, which was across from his grandmother's, so Arleta could use it. He would be sleeping upstairs in the unfinished loft. When he returned to the kitchen, Arleta was standing on her tiptoes, pulling mugs from the cupboard.

"Don't worry, I've washed my hands," she informed him, as if reading his mind.

"I hope you understand that even a common cold could turn into pneumonia for my *groossmammi*—"

"I *do* understand. And I'll be careful to keep everything extra clean."

As Arleta turned to him and smiled, exposing a little space between her otherwise perfectly aligned front teeth, something about her seemed pleasantly familiar. She'd said she came to New Hope for the house building, but his memories of that day were foggy at best. Was it possible they'd crossed paths in Serenity Ridge more recently when Noah went there to finalize his partnership with the Blank brothers? She'd told him she didn't have any relatives in New Hope, but maybe she had friends here and Noah had seen her in church when she'd come to visit them.

For all he knew, she could have been visiting a

long-distance suitor; she seemed about the same age as some of Noah's slightly younger peers. *If she's not being courted already, I imagine there will be a few men vying to be her suitor once they meet her.* The thought unsettled Noah, primarily because he didn't want anything to distract Arleta from helping his grandmother recover.

He lowered his voice to say, "My *groossmammi* is going to tell you not to fret so much, but her doctors said her immune system is like a newborn *bobbel*'s."

Noah crossed the room to remove a notebook from a drawer by the sink. He had intended to review its contents with Arleta before his grandmother woke up, but since Arleta arrived late, he didn't get the opportunity. He didn't want Sovilla to overhear him, so he put the notebook on the countertop.

"This contains important information, like my *groossmammi*'s medication list and her doctor's phone number. The shanty is about two miles south of us—you probably noticed it on your way here. But if you cut straight through the woods out back, you can reach Moses Schrock's feed and grain store. He has a cell phone for business purposes, so if there's an emergency—"

A horn interrupted him. Mike had just tapped on it gently, but Noah was irked. What if his grandmother had been sleeping? It was vital that she got enough rest.

"Don't worry. I'll read through the entire notebook. And there won't be an emergency," Arleta said. Then, because no one could have made such a promise, she added, "*Gott* willing."

Noah should have been reassured by her confidence that everything would be okay, but as he headed outside to get into his coworker's truck, all he could do was pray that she was right.

Chapter Two

As Arleta watched Noah lope across the lawn, she silently prayed, *Please, Gott, give him peace of mind about my taking care of his groossmammi.*

From the first moment he greeted her, Arleta had been struck by Noah's brown eyes, which seemed especially large, no doubt because his rectangular-shaped face was so thin. Anyone looking at it might have thought *he* was the one who was recovering from a long illness. At least his tall, sinewy physique appeared healthy, and his dark mane of hair was even thicker than Arleta remembered it being when she'd met him at the house building.

Well, she hadn't actually *met* him. She'd been serving lemonade, and someone commented that they hadn't seen him around. So, with a full glass in hand, Arleta went off to find him. She'd searched everywhere with no success, and she'd almost given up when she wiggled open the door to the little workshop behind the house. He'd been sitting on the workbench, his head bowed. At first she thought he was praying, but when he glanced up there were tears in his eyes and the expression on his face was one of bewildered anguish. Almost as if he was wondering, *How did I get here?*

"I—I'm sorry," Arleta had stuttered, feeling bad for intruding on his privacy. "I thought you might be thirsty."

She'd extended the glass to him, and although he lifted his hand to accept it, he didn't say anything before dropping his chin to his chest again, his face obscured by his hat. Turning, she'd quietly exited the workshop so he could have his solitude.

His expression when she mentioned the house building today wasn't nearly as distraught as it was when she'd walked in on him in the workshop, but there was an undeniable sadness in his eyes and she wished she hadn't brought it up. Especially because he'd been so quick to change the subject. *I'll have to remember to bridle my tongue.*

When she went into the living room to serve Sovilla a cup of coffee, she found the old woman reclining on the sofa, snoring softly. Since she'd said she was frequently cold, Arleta pulled the folded quilt from the back of the couch and covered her with it. Then she tiptoed into the kitchen and read through the notebook.

As Noah mentioned, it contained a medication list, including the dosages and times his grandmother was supposed to take her pills. There were doctors' names and phone numbers and printouts from the hospital regarding patient nutrition, sleep and exercise during the recovery period. There was also a leaflet about caring for someone with a compromised immune system. Arleta read through all of it twice and paid special attention to the section about preventing additional illness and watching for signs of infection.

Sovilla was still sleeping when Arleta finished, so she went into the basement to begin washing the laundry. Sarah Troyer must not have been able to get to it for a while because there were several baskets of dirty clothes and bedding sitting by the wringer. By the time Arleta had hung everything out to dry, Sovilla was stirring. Arleta brought her a glass of water and took a seat on the chair opposite her.

"It sure is a beautiful spring day," Arleta said conversationally, allowing Sovilla time to open her eyes and adjust to being awake. "I noticed your daffodils have almost finished blooming, but the tulips are beginning to open now."

"I'd like to get out and see them. Sarah, the *weibsmensch* who was here before you, didn't take me outside very often. She always had some excuse. First it was her allergies. Then she said she was too tired because she was with child. She was a dear *weibsmensch* but a *baremlich* fibber. It wasn't her fault—I'm sure Noah convinced her I'd keel over if I went out into the sunlight."

Sovilla gave a little chuckle, but Arleta's concern must have registered on her face because the older woman quickly added, "I *won't* keel over. Not from the sunshine anyway."

This time, Arleta smiled. Sovilla's outlook was the opposite of Noah's, just as he'd told her it would be.

"That's *gut*. But I don't want you to faint from hunger, either. It's almost noon. Is there something in particular you'd like me to make for lunch?"

"What does the notebook say I'm allowed to eat?" Sovilla asked wryly.

"I—I," Arleta stammered, unsure whether Noah would have wanted her to acknowledge that he'd given her an instructional notebook about his grandmother's care.

Sovilla's eyes twinkled. "It's okay, dear. I was pulling your leg. But I am aware Noah keeps a list of my dos and don'ts. I never pay it any mind."

Relieved, Arleta laughed. She appreciated Sovilla's sense of humor and independence. "I'll make some *supp*, then. I saw leftover *hinkel* in the fridge. Will that be all right?"

"You can fix whatever you like for meals, as long as you're not insulted if I don't always eat what you prepare. I don't have a big appetite anymore. The medication altered my sense of taste so I don't relish food like I used to… Although I can't imagine not enjoying a sliver of bumbleberry pie if someone were to make it for me," Sovilla hinted.

"I won't be insulted," Arleta assured her. But as she recalled that the pamphlet said it was important for cancer patients to keep their weight up, she silently made it her mission to come up with a nutritious meal plan that would appeal to Sovilla. Including the occasional treat. "As it happens, pies are my specialty. So if you get a craving for one, just let me know."

Sovilla gave a satisfied smile before closing her eyes

and leaning her head back against the cushion again. "Didn't I say we'd get along like two peas in a pod?"

Jah—*but I'm not sure that's going to make Noah as* hallich *as it makes you,* Arleta worried to herself as she rose and went into the kitchen.

At noon, as the men scrambled down off the roof of the house they were working on to take their lunch break, Mike mentioned he had to run to the bank.

"Since you're driving past my place anyway, can you drop me off and then pick me up on your way back?" Noah asked, and Mike readily agreed.

"Your lunch breaks are so quick you're usually done eating before the rest of us have unwrapped our sandwiches," David remarked. "Why are you going all the way home—is everything okay with your *groossmammi*?"

"I think she's fine but I want to check in on her."

"Is it really your *groossmammi* you're checking on, or is it the *maedel* you hired from Serenity Ridge you want to see?" Mike ribbed him.

"That's right, she arrived this morning, didn't she?" Jacob chimed in. He had recently reached courting age and was more outspoken about his interest in girls than many of his Amish peers. Which wasn't to say they weren't interested, too, only that they kept their thoughts to themselves, especially in front of adults David's age. "What's she like? Is she pretty?"

Noah shrugged. "I didn't notice, either way."

"Did you meet her when you picked Noah up this morning?" Jacob asked Mike.

"Nope, but I'll try to this afternoon," Mike taunted.

"*Neh*, you won't," Noah gruffly interjected. "Your boots are crawling with germs. You're not coming into my *haus* wearing those."

"He can take them off." Sometimes Jacob didn't know when enough was enough and Noah had to remind himself to be patient. The teenager had been orphaned as a toddler and raised by his grandmother and great-aunt, so he hadn't grown up with a man in the house to help him mature. "And then he can tiptoe across the floor in his bare feet."

"His feet probably are dirtier than his boots," David suggested, causing Jacob to crack up.

"They may not be dirtier, but they're definitely smellier," Mike admitted good-naturedly.

As Noah and Mike walked toward the truck, Noah reflected on how grateful he was to have found a Christian *Englischer* like him to join their team. Although he was a little rough around the edges, his generosity, skill and dedication more than made up for it.

A few minutes later when Mike dropped him off, Noah said, "I'll be watching for you to return. No need to honk—you'll wake up my *groossmammi* if she's napping."

"She's already awake." Mike pointed to the side of the house where Arleta and Sovilla were walking arm in arm. "So the hired girl's a redhead, huh?"

Noah bristled at Mike's reference to *the hired girl.* "Arleta," he said.

"Huh?"

"The young woman I hired is named Arleta. And

her hair is more blonde than red." The words were out of Noah's mouth before he realized he'd spoken them aloud. He opened the door and hopped out of the truck.

"Not that you noticed, right?" Mike chortled as Noah shoved the door shut.

"What are you doing out here?" he asked when he got close enough that he didn't have to shout. It wasn't that the doctor prohibited his grandmother from going outdoors, but Noah wished she wouldn't. He'd had a raccoon problem that spring, and he didn't want his grandmother to inadvertently come into contact with their droppings, which he'd heard could transmit diseases to people.

"Enjoying the *gut* Lord's creation," Sovilla answered, waving to Mike as he drove away. "What are *you* doing here?"

Noah couldn't tell Sovilla he was checking up on Arleta because it was her first day and he hadn't had time to review his grandmother's care with her. "I came for lunch."

"Oh, *neh*! Did the birds fly away with the sandwich you brought to work with you?" his grandmother needled him. He should have known better than to try to pull one over on her.

Fortunately, Arleta cut in. "I've got *supp* simmering on the stove. It must be ready by now and I'm *hungerich*, too. Let's go eat."

His grandmother linked her other arm through Noah's and the three of them shambled so slowly to the house that Noah was concerned Mike would circle back before the trio even made it inside. Finally, they took their shoes off at the door.

"I'm so spent I doubt I can make it down the hall to wash my hands," Sovilla admitted.

That's another reason why it's a bad idea for you to go outside. You need to conserve your energy, Noah thought. He'd have to talk to Arleta about this once his grandmother was out of earshot.

"That's okay. There's no hurry. You can rest a minute, and then we can wash our hands in the kitchen sink and Noah can use the bathroom to wash his," Arleta said.

When he returned, his grandmother was sitting at the table and her cheeks were pink, probably from overexertion. "Are you okay, *Groossmammi*? Your face is red."

"That's because I got my blood circulating for once," Sovilla said with a laugh.

"You overdid it. I wish you wouldn't—"

Sovilla cut him off. "Every day for the past two weeks, you've told me how pale I look. Now I've finally got a little color and you're concerned about that, too. I'm fine, *suh*. You must stop worrying. Arleta is taking *gut* care of me, aren't you, Arleta?"

Arleta turned from the stove. "As best as I can," she said diplomatically and edged toward the table balancing a full bowl of soup.

By exhausting her with a walk around the yard? Noah wondered as she set the soup down in front of him.

Then she served a smaller bowl for Sovilla and one for herself. For the first few moments after Noah said grace, no one spoke as they sipped spoonsful of the hot, savory liquid. Noah was heartened to see his grand-mother trying the broth; lately her diet consisted of crackers and ginger tea. Actually, his diet hadn't been very healthy, either. Sarah routinely fixed something for him to eat for supper, but eating alone in the evening really seemed to put a dent in his appetite.

"It's *gut*," he mumbled.

"I'm glad you like it, because we'll be eating it for a while," Arleta replied. "I'm so used to cooking for my *familye*, I made way too much."

"How many *brieder* and *schweschdere* do you have?" Noah asked.

"Four *brieder* and one *schweschder*."

"That's not so many. I thought you were going to say you had nine or ten siblings."

"I might as well have, the way my *brieder* eat. I think they consume half their body weight in food during each meal," she remarked, causing Noah to chuckle.

"A *gut* appetite is a sign of *gut* health," Sovilla said.

"If that's true, they should live to be as old as Methu-selah," Arleta joked. "I don't begrudge them their appe-tites and I enjoy cooking for them. I just wish sometimes they'd leave a crumb or two for the rest of us. Noah, you're fortunate you don't have *brieder* like mine—"

Arleta must have realized what she'd said because she abruptly stopped talking, which Noah felt was bet-ter for everyone. Unfortunately, his grandmother didn't drop the subject.

"Noah had two *brieder* and one *schweschder*, didn't you?" Sovilla prompted.

Noah nodded and ducked his head over his bowl,

quickly filling his mouth with food so he wouldn't have
to speak.

"His *daed*, Elmo, was my only *suh*. My only *kind*, in
fact. That's how I came to be in Maine—I moved here
from Michigan with Elmo's *familye*," Sovilla explained.

"That's a big move. Do you ever go back to Michigan to visit?" Arleta asked.

"I used to go once a year, when my *schweschder* was
still alive. I was actually visiting her when the fire occurred, otherwise—"

"I think I hear Mike," Noah said, standing. Even
though it had been six years since the fire, he didn't understand how his grandmother could speak so matter-
of-factly about it—or speak about it at all. What's more,
he didn't want Arleta to ask where *he'd* been the night
of the fire. As he strode out of the house, he said over
his shoulder, more to Arleta than to his grandmother,
"Make sure to take it easy this afternoon."

What is wrong with me, making a joke about my
brieder *living to be as old as Methuselah and telling
Noah he's fortunate he doesn't have any* brieder *like
mine?* Arleta silently chastised herself. *He'd probably give his eyeteeth to have his* familye *back again.* It
was abundantly obvious Noah didn't like to talk about
his family, yet the harder Arleta tried to censor herself
from saying anything about them or the fire, the more
she slipped up.

Sovilla, on the other hand, was eager to tell Arleta
stories about her son and his family. As she took a stroll
down memory lane, Arleta listened intently. She wanted

to honor the older woman's desire to reminisce about her loved ones as much as she wanted to respect Noah's desire not to mention them at all. Arleta had only been here a few hours and already she could feel the tension between their two personalities. They weren't unkind toward each other—on the contrary, their mutual affection was obvious—but they were *so* different. It was going to be tricky for Arleta to appease them both.

After she'd entertained Arleta with several family anecdotes, Sovilla peppered her with questions about her own family. Finally, she yawned and asked Arleta to help her down the hall. "I need to take another nap. A real nap this time—in my bed, not on the sofa."

Arleta extended her arm and forced a smile even though she felt like weeping. In addition to upsetting Noah with her remarks, she'd tuckered Sovilla out completely. What a fine help she was! After she assisted Sovilla into bed and arranged her pillows, she turned to leave but the older woman grasped her hand.

"Look at me and tell me what's troubling you."

Arleta hardly knew Sovilla and she was supposed to be here to comfort her, not the other way around. "Nothing's wrong."

"You're as bad of a fibber as Sarah was," Sovilla scolded. "Is it that I didn't finish my *supp*?"

"*Neh*, of course not," Arleta protested before she realized Sovilla was only teasing in order to try to trick her into saying what was really on her mind.

"Then what is it? Hurry and tell me, *kind*, or I won't be able to sleep and I'm so drowsy."

"I feel *baremlich* for…for having such a big *moul*

and upsetting Noah and for wearing you out on my first day here."

"Ach! You didn't wear me out. I always rest at this time of day. Wasn't that written down in the notebook?" Sovilla gave her an impish wink. "As for anything you said to Noah, don't worry about it. You didn't intend to upset him, just as he didn't intend to insult you by asking if your socks were clean."

"Oh, that didn't insult me. I know he's only concerned about germs because he doesn't want you to get sick."

"Exactly. Likewise, he knows you were just making a joke about your *brieder*." Sovilla released Arleta's fingers and patted the top of her hand. "He's *hallich* you're here and so am I."

Arleta wasn't quite sure she believed that. In fact, she was beginning to think coming here was a big mistake. She returned to the kitchen and as she cleaned up, she thought about how she and Leanna sometimes used to sing during their chores. Now, she hummed quietly to herself. Arleta hadn't even been here a full day and already she felt homesick. At times like these, she wondered how she ever considered permanently leaving her family and community.

She knew the answer: little by little, she'd crossed the boundaries that separated the Amish from the *Englisch*, and right from wrong. It began with her thoughts and soon, her actions followed until... Arleta glanced down at her feet. She was surprised to notice a ring of dirt around her sock near her ankle. How had she missed seeing that? How had *Noah* missed seeing that?

She went into her room and quietly opened her suitcase. She took out a clean pair of socks. Peeling off her dirty ones, she examined her tattoo. In dimmer light, she could fool herself into believing the heart was fading, but not today when the sunshine was streaming through the windows. *What is it Ephesians says about every sinful thing is made manifest in the light?* Arleta shook her head and quickly pulled a fresh sock over her ankle.

As she put the rest of her clothing away, she silently quoted another Bible verse, 1 John 1:9, which said, *If we confess our sins, he is faithful and just to forgive us our sins, and to cleanse us from all unrighteousness.* Reciting God's promise comforted Arleta, who wholeheartedly believed the Lord had forgiven her for the things she'd done during her *rumspringa*, after she'd confessed them to Him.

However, confessing her wrongdoings to other people and having them forgive her was another matter. Arleta reflected on the time she'd almost told Stephen Yoder about her tattoo. Stephen had come from Canada to visit his relatives in Serenity Ridge the summer after Arleta's baptism, and he'd asked to walk out with her. She'd tentatively agreed and by the end of August, he wanted to know if she'd be willing to continue a long-distance courtship with the intention of getting married when they were twenty-one.

Aware she couldn't carry on a serious courtship—much less, get married—without being honest about her tattoo, Arleta worked up the courage to ask Stephen if he'd ever done anything he regretted during his *rumspringa*.

"*Jah.* Hasn't everyone?" he'd freely admitted, causing Arleta's heart to soar with hope that maybe he wouldn't judge her after all.

"If I promise not to tell a soul, will you tell me the thing you did that you regret most?"

So Stephen had confessed he'd climbed a water tower and spray-painted a love message to a girl on it. Apparently, the note wasn't from him but from an *Englischer* who was too scared to climb the tower himself. Since Stephen was used to climbing silo ladders, he did it for him.

"That's it? That's the worst thing?" Arleta had understood why he'd feel ashamed for defacing someone else's property, but she didn't think what he'd done was anywhere near as terrible as what she'd done. Especially since he'd gotten caught and had to repay the water company to repaint the tower.

"*Jah.* Why, what was the worst thing you did on *rumspringa?*"

Arleta wished she'd never brought up the subject. "It's much worse than what you did. You might not want to be my suitor once I tell you," she reluctantly admitted.

"I can't imagine anything changing the way I feel about you."

"Well, I…" She'd hemmed and hawed. "I guess you could say I kind of did something along the lines of graffiti, too. But what I wrote can't be painted over."

His eyes had gone wide. "Why not?"

Arleta had taken a deep breath and said, "Because it's on my skin. I—I got a tattoo."

He'd paused, his mouth dropping open before he hooted and slapped his knee. "*Voll schpass!* I almost thought you were serious."

"I *am* serious." She'd been on the brink of taking off her shoe and sock to prove it to him, but his expression suddenly turned hard.

"Arleta Bontrager, you can't be serious. *Meed* don't do such things. At least, not any *maedel* I'd ever court."

Arleta had felt like sobbing, but instead, she began to laugh in order to make Stephen think she'd been joking all along. For two months afterward, she'd kept up a long-distance courtship, too. Not because she had any interest in marrying him after that, but because she was scared if she ended the relationship right after their conversation, he'd realize why. He'd realize she'd been serious about her tattoo and he'd tell everyone. They'd all know the shameful things she'd done. They'd know she'd been planning to leave…

As she stowed her suitcase in the closet, Arleta realized she'd been covering one sin with another. For the past two years, she'd been hiding her tattoo with deception, just as surely as she'd been hiding it with a sock. She couldn't stand being so dishonest. *That's another reason I have to get Ian's initials removed*, she told herself. Which meant that no matter how much she doubted whether she was being helpful here and no matter how homesick she felt, she couldn't leave. No, unless Noah outright fired her, Arleta was there to stay.

The crew completed the roof installation and managed to pick up the debris and collect their tools just before five thirty. On the way home, Noah used Mike's cell phone to call Colin Blank's business phone. They discussed the next project, which was closer to Noah's home than the one they'd just finished. The next day, Mike was going to take the measurements, cut the sheeting and edging, and deliver everything from their local workshop to the site while the other men removed the old roofing and repaired any damaged areas they found.

However, Noah wanted to check if there were any small installations he could work on in the upcoming week, like roofing for a mobile home. He figured even if the other men didn't choose to work extra hours, he'd be able to handle a small project himself. Sure enough, Colin had a backlog of New Hope orders. Noah chose to start with a shed roof for an *Englischer* whose home was located right down the street from where Noah lived.

Approaching his house, he was surprised to see all the windows opened—usually his grandmother complained she was too cold. The smell of onions wafted through the air.

"Hello," he said to Arleta as he removed his boots at the door.

She was stirring something in the frying pan and she momentarily glanced over her shoulder to reply, "Hi, Noah. Supper will be ready in about ten minutes."

"*Gut.* That will give me time to clean up." Before heading to the bathroom, he peeked into the living room to greet his grandmother. Arleta must have spied him from the corner of her eye because she told him Sovilla wasn't there; she was in her bedroom.

"Please don't open her door."

Noah's heart thudded. Was his grandmother still winded from her walk this afternoon? "Why not? Is she sleeping?"

"*Neh.* She doesn't feel *gut.* She told me I could make anything I wanted to, so I made beef and noodle casserole. The recipe called for half a chopped onion, and the smell of it frying made her nauseated."

As Arleta looked at him, her eyes were watery and Noah wasn't sure whether it was from the onions or if she was on the brink of tears.

Noah certainly didn't want her to cry, but he also wished his grandmother didn't feel sick to her stomach. He didn't know what else to say except, "Oh, I see."

Arleta turned back to the stove and continued stirring, so he went into the bathroom. When he was through washing his hands and face, he returned to find her putting the salt and pepper shakers on the table. Wearing a slight frown, she wordlessly took her seat and Noah did, too. They bowed their heads for grace.

"*Denki, Gott,* for this food. Please strengthen us with it. Strengthen *Groossmammi,* too, Lord. Give her healing from the cancer and relief from the nausea." He ended by saying, "And *denki* for sending Arleta to help us during this time. Amen."

Opening his eyes, Noah noticed a change in Arleta's demeanor. She wasn't smiling, but she wasn't frowning anymore, either. She seemed…*lighter,* somehow, as she went to the stove and scooped a big helping of casserole onto his plate and then half as much on hers.

"Are you sure you have enough?" he asked genially,

relieved that she no longer seemed on the verge of tears. "I don't want to be accused of not leaving a crumb for you."

She looked taken aback, but then she must have realized he was making a joke in reference to what she'd said about her brothers and she smiled. "I don't think there's any danger of that, especially since your *groossmammi* isn't joining us for supper. I cut the recipe in half, but we're still going to have leftovers."

"That's okay. I can stick them in my cooler and eat them for lunch tomorrow."

"Cold?"

"Hot, cold or lukewarm, it makes no difference to me—I love beef casserole."

"That's too bad, because this is the last time I can make it for you," Arleta said. "I don't want to make your *groossmammi* ill again."

The sincere concern in her voice mirrored the apprehension in her eyes. Studying her, Noah realized she really was trying her best to keep his grandmother comfortable and well. He found himself saying, "It's okay. You didn't know it would affect her like that. *She* probably didn't even know, because Sarah hasn't made any food with onions in it since *Groossmammi*'s last treatment. I'm the one who bought onions and put them in the pantry, so if anyone is to blame, it's me."

"Blame for what?" Sovilla said from where she leaned against the doorframe, hugging a shawl to her chest.

"For the *schtinke*," Noah answered.

Arleta jumped up and began shutting the windows. "You must be cold. If you go sit by the stove, I'll bring you a cup of ginger tea."

"I will go sit by the stove, but I don't want any tea. I'm *hungerich*. I'd like to try some of that casserole after all."

Arleta cocked her head to one side. "Are you sure?"

"*Jah*. Just bring it to me in a bowl, please." Sovilla shuffled into the living room.

"I'm relieved she's feeling so much better." Arleta stretched to try to reach a bowl from the cupboard.

"Here, I'll get that for you," Noah offered. She stepped aside so he could retrieve the dish. Even so, as he pulled down a bowl he was acutely aware that he hadn't stood this close to a single woman since he'd courted Hannah Miller. Come to think of it, he hadn't spent this much time conversing with a single woman, either.

Then it dawned on him: *Groossmammi wasn't really that ill! She wanted Arleta and me to have to eat together without her. She was giving us privacy so we could get to know each other better.* And that was why she'd retreated into the living room now, too. Or was it? He couldn't be sure. Not that it mattered. Even if his grandmother was scheming to match him and Arleta, Noah wasn't going to develop a romantic relationship with her or with anyone else. How could the Lord entrust him with a new family when Noah had been so irresponsible toward the family he'd already had? No, his interest in Arleta was solely as his grandmother's caretaker.

But that didn't mean Noah didn't notice what a sweet, gap-toothed smile she gave him when he handed her the bowl.

Chapter Three

Once Arleta and Noah discussed the guidelines for his grandmother's care and home environment and after a few days had passed, Arleta felt increasingly confident in her ability to keep Sovilla well and the household environment healthy. Noah must have felt more confident in her abilities, too, because on Wednesday, Thursday and Friday evenings, he worked late. Which meant Sovilla was the only person Arleta saw for most of the day, since Noah told Arleta he'd put the word out that his grandmother shouldn't have visitors.

Actually, Arleta didn't see all that much of Sovilla, either, since the elderly woman slept off and on throughout the late morning and again in the afternoon. Arleta spent that time cleaning the house, doing the laundry and making meals, just as she would have done at home. She also transferred seedlings and tended the vegetable garden and flower beds. Noah had insisted on taking care of the animals and cleaning the coop and stable himself. Arleta realized he was probably concerned she'd track something into the house, which was slightly offensive, considering how meticulous she was. But she could just imagine Leanna telling her she was crazy to argue with him if it meant she got out of the unappealing chore, so she didn't. Arleta had plenty of time left over for reading, and she even composed a letter to her sister.

She was grateful that she was being compensated handsomely for work that wasn't nearly as arduous as what she did in her own home. And when Sovilla was awake, Arleta genuinely enjoyed her company. But sometimes, while Sovilla was dozing, Arleta would find herself thinking, *This is how it will be for me at home in another ten years once my* brieder *and* schweschder *have all gotten married and moved away and* mamm *and* daed *are older.* But that wasn't necessarily true; she could count on at least one or two of her siblings and their spouses and children residing in her parents' house at some point. That's what she hoped, anyway, because this kind of quietness didn't seem natural to her and she was getting restless.

So on Friday evening when Noah asked if she'd rather take the buggy and go to town for groceries the next morning or make up a list and have him get the food, she jumped at the chance to go shopping herself.

"She doesn't know the way," Sovilla pointed out. "Why would you send her off alone?"

"Because it will give you and me a chance to visit," Noah replied.

"Pah. You're just afraid to leave me on my own," Sovilla responded, and Arleta knew she was right. Then she added, "But this is one time I don't mind if you treat me like a feeble old lady. I've missed seeing your face. You've been keeping awfully late hours at work."

"I've told you, *Groossmammi*, this is the busiest time of the year for installations. If we don't keep up with the demand, we'll lose customers."

Sovilla clicked her tongue against her teeth. "Even so, I'm surprised Colin Blank expects his crew to spend evenings apart from their *familye*. He ought to care more about the people under his employees' roofs than putting new roofs on *Englischers'* homes."

Arleta noticed a pained look cross Noah's face, and she wondered if he was keeping something from his grandmother. She couldn't imagine what it would be but she interjected, "I don't mind going alone. Most men I know get impatient in the grocery store. This way, I can take my time without worrying about Noah pacing the aisles."

"Uh, I'd actually appreciate it if you'd *kumme* back as soon as you can. I'll need the buggy because tomorrow I'm starting a new project a few miles from here."

"You're working on *Samschdaag*, after all the extra hours you already put in this week?" Sovilla was incredulous.

"I'm sorry, *Groossmammi*, but the *Englischer* whose roof I'm installing wants to be there while I'm working on it. He's at his own job during the rest of the week, so—"

"*Englischer* this, *Englischer* that. If you keep allowing the *Englisch* to influence you, pretty soon you'll be working on *Sunndaag*, too."

"You know me better than that, *Groossmammi*. I'd never do something like compromise the Sabbath because of any *Englischer*'s influence." Noah's cheeks and ears flushed bright red.

Sovilla was quiet for a moment before she acknowledged, "*Neh*, I know you wouldn't, *suh*. I'm sorry."

Noah rubbed his forehead and released a heavy sigh. "It's okay, *Groossmammi*. You're right. I have been working a lot, and I'm going to have to keep up this pace for a while. But I really *am* looking forward to having a quiet *Sunndaag* together."

Then, since she said she wasn't quite tired yet, Sovilla suggested they play a three-person version of spades. Although the tension between her and her grandson had lifted, their remarks ate at Arleta. Sovilla was right, of course; it was important to guard against the practices and temptations of the *Englisch* world. But it hurt to imagine what she might have thought of Arleta if she knew how much *she'd* once been influenced by an *Englisch* boy.

And Noah's disgust at his grandmother's suggestion that he might violate his faith and work on the Sabbath really struck a nerve. He sounded so appalled it reminded Arleta of Stephen's tone when he said, "*Meed* don't do such things. At least, not any *maedel* I'd ever court."

While Arleta didn't blame Noah for being indignant, his assertion that he'd never compromise his beliefs underscored the secret fact that Arleta *had* compromised hers. *If Noah knew about my tattoo—or about the other things I did—would he ask me to leave?* Beneath the table, she self-consciously pulled her feet closer to her chair. After Sovilla won the game and asked if they wanted to play again, Arleta declined, saying she was tired. Then she retreated to her room.

It was warm enough to sleep with the windows open and a quilt was no longer necessary, either. Since she had the room to herself and she didn't have to worry about Leanna seeing her ankle, it was probably safe for Arleta to go to bed barefoot. It certainly would have been cooler. *But what if Sovilla needs me in the middle of the night?* she wondered. Arleta had already accepted the fact that her tattoo—as well as planning to leave the Amish—had cost her a future as a wife, but she didn't want it to cost her a job, too. So she reluctantly donned a fresh pair of socks, removed her prayer *kapp* and went to bed.

By the time she set out for the grocery store the next morning, the sting of Sovilla's and Noah's remarks had subsided. For one thing, she felt a sense of adventure, exploring a new town. For another, she was anticipating buying ingredients for a couple of interesting recipes she'd found in Sovilla's recipe box.

New Hope's Amish population was large enough that part of the store's parking lot was reserved for buggies only. Arleta had just loaded her purchases into the back of the carriage when another buggy pulled up alongside her and a young woman got out.

"My name's Faith Smoker," she said, introducing herself. "You must be the *maedel* staying with Sovilla— I recognize Noah's *gaul*."

"*Jah*. I'm Arleta Bontrager."

"How is Sovilla?"

"She seems to be getting stronger each day."

"Is she ready for visitors?" Faith asked. "Or maybe I should ask if Noah is ready to allow her to have visitors?"

Arleta bit back a smile. "I'm not sure."

"*You're* probably ready for visitors, though. You must not get to see many other people."

"That's true, I don't. But I really enjoy Sovilla's company."

"Ach. I didn't mean to imply you didn't. Sometimes I really stick my foot in my *moul*," Faith said, and Arleta could empathize since she had a tendency to misspeak, too. "I was only thinking aloud about your situation because some of us are going on a hike through the woods and then having a picnic tomorrow after *kurrich*. There will be a few *buwe* and a few *meed*, all around our age. You're *wilkom* to join us. It's supposed to be a beautiful day."

"Oh, that sounds like *schpass*! But I'll have to talk it over with Sovilla and Noah, first."

"Tell Noah he should *kumme*, too."

Arleta's initial exuberance quickly faded. If Noah wanted to go, that meant she would have to stay behind with Sovilla. Although she recognized that's what she'd been hired to do and she truly did like spending time with Noah's grandmother, Arleta wasn't used to being indoors with only one other person for such a long stretch of time. *Maybe Noah will decide he'd rather be the one to stay home*, she thought hopefully.

She intended to tell him about the invitation as soon

as she arrived home, but he was in such a hurry to get to work she'd barely carried the bags inside when he shot out the door in the opposite direction.

"Did you meet anyone in town?" Sovilla asked, coming into the kitchen to chat while Arleta put the food away. Arleta had reorganized Sovilla's cupboards so she could reach everything—Noah and his grandmother were much taller than she was—but now the lower shelves were so full she barely had enough room for the new items. She stood on tiptoes to put a can of tuna fish on an upper shelf.

"*Jah.* I met Faith Smoker."

"Ah, Faith. Her *familye* was one of the first to move to New Hope. She's lived here since she was in *windel.*" Even though they were alone in the house, Sovilla lowered her voice to confide, "Her *mamm* always expected the community would have grown more by now. She's worried her *dochder* doesn't have enough choices for a suitor. But I heard from Sarah that Faith has her sights set on Jacob Auer, the young man who works with Noah."

"Oh, maybe that's why—" She caught herself, but Sovilla prodded her to finish her sentence. Arleta hadn't wanted to tell her about the picnic until after she'd spoken to Noah about it, but she didn't have a choice. "Faith invited me to go on a hike after *kurrich.* She invited Noah, too—along with a few other young people. I imagine Jacob will be one of them."

It wasn't acceptable for an Amish woman to initiate a courtship with an Amish man, but some women found ways to let the men know they were interested, including inviting them to group activities. Arleta suspected that was why Faith had arranged the hike with her peers.

"Wunderbaar!" Sovilla exclaimed, clasping her hands beneath her chin. "This is exactly what Noah needs. A little *schpass* with people his own age."

Arleta bent down to pull a box from the canvas bag so Sovilla wouldn't see how disappointed she felt that Noah would be going on the picnic and Arleta wouldn't. But Sovilla surprised her by adding, "And it will be *wunderbaar* for you to go out with the youth, too. Maybe you'll even find a suitor among the *buwe* of New Hope."

"I don't think that's a *gut* idea," Arleta argued, knowing Noah wouldn't want Sovilla to be left alone for the afternoon.

"Why not? Are you courting someone at home?"

"Neh, but that's not why I don't think it will be a *gut* idea…" It was one thing for Noah to risk insulting his grandmother by saying she shouldn't be left alone, but Arleta didn't dare suggest it herself.

"Noah isn't courting anyone, either," Sovilla babbled on. "Can you believe he hasn't walked out with a *meed* since he was seventeen? I keep telling him there's more to life than working and sitting at home at night with his *groossmammi*."

Noah hadn't courted anyone since he was seventeen? This piece of information surprised Arleta. Not that it was any of her business, but it struck her as strange. Noah might not have been the most cheerful man she'd ever met, but he was hardworking, thoughtful and kind. And devoted to his grandmother, a trait Arleta found especially endearing. Not to mention, he was tall and strong and had pretty eyes. Any of her friends in Serenity Ridge would have lined up to court him. And at one time, Arleta would have lined up with them.

She figured Sovilla must have been right: Noah didn't court anyone because he spent all his time working or with her. While his sense of responsibility was admirable, it seemed a pity he hadn't had the opportunity to court a woman in over six years. Arleta knew from her own experience how lonely it felt not to have the hope of a romantic relationship, and she empathized. *Maybe now that I'm here around the clock, he'll be able to go out during the evenings on occasion.*

"This picnic might be the nudge he needs," Sovilla said. "He'll see what he's been missing for the past six years and he'll enjoy himself so much he'll take time to get out more often."

"*Jah.* But the challenge will be convincing him he should go in the first place." *Especially since he's not going to want to leave you alone for several hours.*

With a glint in her eye, Sovilla replied, "Just leave that to me."

On Sunday morning at breakfast, Sovilla turned to Arleta and said, "Tell Noah about Faith Smoker's invitation for this afternoon."

Arleta swallowed a bite of scrambled eggs and coughed before answering. "She and a few other people are going hiking after *kurrich.* Then we'll have a picnic for supper. I made plenty of potato salad and fried *hinkel* to share."

Noah was a little surprised that Arleta hadn't discussed spending the afternoon away from the house before putting her plans into motion. What if he'd had someone to visit and needed her to stay with Sovilla? Then he realized he'd mentioned that he'd been looking forward to spending a quiet Sabbath with his grandmother. Besides, he could understand why Arleta was eager to hang out with younger people for a change.

He smiled and remarked, "I hope you have *schpass*."

"Faith invited you, too, Noah," Sovilla told him.

"That's nice, but I don't want to go. You and I are going to have a nice, restful afternoon together, *Groossmammi*, remember?"

"*Suh*, I appreciate it that you want to keep me company, but to tell you the truth, I'd prefer to go to Lovina Bawell's *haus* for the afternoon," his grandmother said. "It's been two weeks since I got out of the hospital, so I don't have to keep isolated any longer."

"But Lovina has six of her *kinskind* living in her *haus*. You heard what the *dokder* said about avoiding small *kinner* for at least a month."

As it was, because Sovilla's immune system was compromised, she should have been avoiding large gatherings, such as for church, too, but Noah had already lost that battle. Sovilla had told him she didn't care if she had to crawl to church on her knees; nothing was going to stop her from worshipping. But at least she'd agreed to wear a protective mask and she didn't mingle after the services.

Sovilla snapped her fingers. "*Jah*, you're right. I suppose Lovina will have to *kumme* here instead. Maybe her *dochder* will *kumme*, too, and we can all play bridge or put together a jigsaw puzzle. Arleta made plenty of chicken and potato salad for us, too. You *kin* can eat your supper on the porch, so Lovina and I can natter away in private in the *haus*."

Inwardly, Noah moaned, recognizing his grandmother had hoodwinked him. Lovina Bawell's youngest daughter, Honor, was a nice enough person, but he knew what it would look like if she found out that he had the opportunity to go hiking and instead he'd stayed home to play games on the afternoon she was invited to visit. His grandmother knew what it would look like, too, and she was using that to her advantage.

"*Neh.* I'd rather go hiking," he glumly conceded. Noah actually used to enjoy hiking on Sundays, but Faith Smoker was barely seventeen years old, and he supposed most of the people she invited would be teenagers, too. People who were just beginning to court and thought of little else. People who were as immature and irresponsible as he was at that age…

"*Gut!* I was hoping you'd want to *kumme*!" Arleta exclaimed, her eyes sparkling. "I'm sure everyone there will be very *freindlich* toward me, but I'll feel more comfortable having you there, too."

She seemed so genuinely happy that Noah smiled, too. But before he could reply, Sovilla said, "*Jah*, once the *buwe* of New Hope find out Arleta isn't being courted, they're going to swarm around her like bees around a hive. Noah, you can watch out for her."

As Arleta dipped her head and scraped the last bits of scrambled eggs from her plate, Noah noticed her ears and the part in her hair that wasn't covered by her prayer *kapp* were turning bright pink. He winced on her behalf. Most young Amish women and men didn't openly discuss whether they were courting anyone, but he surmised his grandmother had wheedled that information out of Arleta. She must have been mortified that Sovilla had announced her courting status in front of Noah like that.

"I—I'm looking forward to the fried *hinkel*," he said, hoping to alleviate Arleta's embarrassment by changing the subject. "Are you bringing some of the whoopie pies you made last night, too?"

Her cheeks were rosy when she raised her head and met his eyes. Even though he knew it was embarrassment that had colored them, he was startled by how becoming she looked. "How many would you like?"

"How many do you have?"

Arleta's face broke into a smile wide enough to expose the little space between her front teeth. Noah was beginning to recognize this as a sign of her authentic amusement. "Nine or ten," she answered.

"Then bring them all."

"Aren't you going to leave a couple for Lovina and me?" Sovilla piped up.

"Lovina's *dochder* can bring dessert for you," Noah suggested, tongue-in-cheek. When he was a teenager, he'd actually chipped a tooth eating a sugar cookie Honor had made—and judging from what she'd brought to recent barn raisings and potlucks, her cooking hadn't improved much since then.

"I'd rather eat onions," Sovilla retorted. To Arleta she

explained, "Honor's a nice *weibsmensch* but a *baremlich* cook."

"I suppose that's better than being a nice cook and a *baremlich weibsmensch*," Arleta said, and all three of them cracked up.

Their shared levity, coupled with Arleta's enthusiasm about the outing, boosted Noah's mood. His grandmother seemed to have a burst of energy, too. *Maybe this will be a* gut *change for all of us*, he thought as they journeyed to church.

New Hope's Amish community, like several of the other Amish settlements in Maine, was unusual in that worship services were held in a church building rather than in a host family's home. They still ate a cold lunch together afterward, so while Arleta was helping clean up, Noah spoke to Lovina's husband, Wayne. The plan was that he would drop the two older women off at Noah's house and Noah would take Lovina home once he returned from the picnic.

"We'll be back as soon as we finish eating supper," he promised his grandmother, who was resting on a bench nearby.

"Don't hurry home on my account. Lovina and I have a lot of catching up to do."

"It's too bad my *dochder* is still visiting her *schweschder* in Ohio. She would have liked to *kumme* with you," Lovina remarked.

Noah recognized the polite thing to do would have been to express disappointment that Honor couldn't make it, but that would have been insincere. He hadn't even noticed whether or not she'd been in church lately, so he asked, "How long has she been in Ohio?"

"It's been over a month now. I'm surprised Soyilla hasn't told you. She's probably getting sick of hearing me gripe about how lonely I've been."

Noah lowered his eyebrows at his grandmother, who was fussing with her kerchief. She'd known all along Lovina's daughter was away! Her threat about inviting Honor to spend the afternoon at their house was an empty one, but it had worked on him. The question was, did she truly want him to go for a hike so she'd have the house to herself to host her friend, or was it because she was pushing him to socialize more? Either way, Noah had to give it to his grandmother; she could outsmart a fox.

After saying goodbye, as he went to look for Arleta, he bumped into Faith, who asked if he and Arleta wanted to ride in her buggy. "I'm taking three others but if we squeeze together, we can all fit. We can circle back to the *kurrich* afterward, and you and Arleta can go home from there."

"*Denki*, but I'll take my own buggy." If the others decided to linger at the park after supper, Noah didn't want to be at the mercy of their schedule. "We're going to park at the gorge, *jah*?"

"*Jah*. I'm going to round everyone up and head out now. We'll meet you two by the trailhead to Pleasant Peak. Arleta was just washing the last few platters. She should be right up."

So Noah went to wait for her at the top of the stairs

leading to the basement, where the kitchen was. He was startled when someone tapped his elbow from behind.

"Waiting for someone?" Arleta gazed up at him. The dress she was wearing was a deep forest green color, and it made her eyes look as bright as spring grass by comparison. She must have gotten hot from working in the kitchen because her forehead and upper lip were dewy with perspiration.

"Noah?" she prompted and he realized he'd been staring.

"*Jah.* I was waiting for you. Everyone else is going to meet us there. I thought you and I should go alone in my buggy." He pivoted toward the exit and then swung back around so quickly he almost knocked into her. "I meant we should go alone because then we can leave when we need to and we don't have to stay as long as everyone else."

Arleta nonchalantly agreed that was a good idea, but Noah felt like a clodhopper, tripping over his words like that. He decided he'd be better off saying nothing than embarrassing himself again. But on the way to the park, Arleta asked him so many questions about the various landmarks they passed that he didn't have any choice but to engage in conversation. The more he talked, the less self-conscious he felt and pretty soon he was regaling Arleta with stories about his childhood escapades with his brothers. Maybe it was the fragrant spring air or the vibrant blue sky or even Arleta's sunny attitude, but reminiscing about his brothers wasn't making him sad the way it usually did.

"See the long stretch of road up ahead? My *brieder* and I used to go skitching there."

"What's skitching?"

"It's hitching a ride from a moving vehicle while you're skating."

Arleta gasped. "You held on to a car while you were wearing rollerblades?"

"*Neh*. We hitched rides from our friends' buggies, not from cars. But they were going pretty fast."

"You were *narrish*! Isn't that illegal?"

"I don't know, but it sure was *dumm*. My youngest *bruder* lost his grip on an incline once. He fell on his backside, chipped his tailbone and broke his wrist."

"Wow. Your *eldre* must have been really upset."

"Not half as upset as the three of us were when we had to pay for my *bruder*'s trip to the emergency room," Noah said.

"Well, your *eldre* probably wanted to teach you a lesson so you wouldn't pull a stunt like that again."

"There was no chance of it happening again. Not because we learned our lesson—but because we had to sell our skates to help cover the medical expenses," Noah explained, making Arleta laugh. When she stopped, he asked, "What kinds of shenanigans did you and your *brieder* get up to when you were a *kind*?"

"Oh, the usual stuff. Jumping across the hay bales on our *onkel*'s farm. Seeing who could slide farthest down the hill in the mud in the pasture. Nothing that was dangerous, just dirty."

"Really? You never did anything reckless when you were growing up?"

"My *brieder* probably did, when I wasn't around. But I didn't."

"Not even on your *rumspringa*?" Noah queried, curious to hear more about Arleta's youth.

From the corner of his eye, Noah saw Arleta shrug. When she didn't answer, he took a longer sideways look at her profile; her cheeks were pink and she was biting her lower lip.

"I sense you're hiding something. Have you got a really *gut* story to tell?" It was unusual for him to banter like this, but then, everything about this afternoon with Arleta was unusual.

"Neh."

"C'mon, please?" He leaned toward her and nudged her elbow with his. "I told you about—"

"Absatz," she said, an edge to her voice.

Noah pulled back. Why was she so hypersensitive about her *rumspringa*? Whatever the reason, he felt like a dolt for getting carried away with his teasing. They rode for a few minutes in awkward silence as he tried to think of a way to smooth things over between them again.

Finally, he asked, "Did Faith mention who else is coming?"

"Jah. Someone named Isaiah Wittmer and your coworker Jacob."

Noah suppressed a groan, imagining all the remarks he'd have to endure at work in the upcoming week once Jacob met Arleta and saw how pretty she was. He'd probably give Noah a hard time for acting as if he hadn't noticed.

"So just the five of us?" he asked.

"*Neh.* She said there would be six…but I can't recall the name of the last person," Arleta said. "Oh, wait, I remember—a *meed* named Hannah."

Noah swallowed. "Hannah Miller?"

When Arleta said yes, it took every ounce of Noah's willpower to keep himself from jumping out of the buggy and sprinting all the way home. Instead, he gritted his teeth and resigned himself to spending the afternoon with the woman he'd been kissing the night his whole world went up in flames.

Chapter Four

Arleta did her best to plaster a smile across her face as she and Noah headed toward the trailhead. Although she realized Noah had only been teasing her about *rumspringa*, his comments underscored how much she regretted her behavior during that period in her life. His innocuous remarks reminded her, once again, that in order to protect her secret she was going to have to be careful to keep her guard up. And not just around him and Sovilla—around other people as well, including the new friends she'd hoped to make.

Suddenly, instead of anticipating the fun she'd have, she just wished she could go back to Sovilla and Noah's house. She would have preferred to spend the afternoon completely alone in her room, writing letters to her mother and Leanna.

"There you are!" Faith called, waving wildly, as if she hadn't seen Arleta and Noah for years.

Although Arleta had glimpsed the others in church, she hadn't had a chance to speak with any of them yet, so Faith made the introductions. On first impression, Arleta figured that Jacob and Faith were the youngest in the group. Hannah appeared closer to her midtwenties and Isaiah seemed around that age, too.

"It's *gut* to finally meet you," Jacob said. "Noah never says a word about you at work. If it weren't that his cooler has been filled with bigger and better lunches, I wouldn't have believed you existed."

Noah never says anything about me? Arleta didn't expect he would have said much about her, but *nothing?* Then, Arleta noticed when Noah greeted Hannah, his face turned red. The tall, thin brunette with bright blue eyes also mumbled a greeting and then quickly glanced away, appearing very self-conscious. Their mutual discomfort was obvious in a way Arleta had recognized between her peers before. While a few Amish youth were open about their romantic interest in each other, far more were discreet. Sometimes, Arleta was actually able to discern whether or not a pair was courting by how *indifferent* they seemed toward each other. So she intuitively gathered that Hannah and Noah might be interested in each other, but didn't want certain other people to know. Which could have explained why Noah had been reluctant to come on the hike in the first place.

It also might have explained why Jacob made a point of announcing that Noah never spoke about Arleta. Maybe Noah had confided his interest in Hannah to the guys at work, so Jacob was emphasizing Noah's disinterest in Arleta for Hannah's benefit. Arleta could certainly understand that—if *she* had been courting or interested in courting a young man and he had a strange young woman living with *his* family, she might feel a bit distrustful, too.

It's not as if Hannah has anything to worry about. Noah would never be interested in someone like me and even if he were, I couldn't reciprocate his affection, she told herself. Or was she jumping to far-fetched conclusions? After all, Sovilla said that Noah hadn't courted since he was seventeen. But it was possible his grandmother didn't *know* he was courting Hannah. Or at least, that he was interested in courting her.

In the event Arleta was right, she decided to give Hannah and Noah as much opportunity as possible to chat with each other alone. Although Arleta couldn't have romance in her life, she certainly didn't want her presence in New Hope to hinder Noah and Hannah from having it in theirs. Especially since Sovilla was so eager to see her grandson develop more of a social life. So, as Jacob and Faith dashed ahead of the group, Arleta struck up a conversation with Isaiah. Because he was over six feet tall, she had to hurry to match his stride, leaving Noah and Hannah to lag behind them.

Arleta commented on the beauty of the gorge, adding that it made her a little nervous to peer over the edge, down to the rocks below. "Even though my town is named after a ridge, I don't think I've ever seen such a steep drop-off," she said.

"What about Paradise Point? That's a really high precipice."

"You've been to Paradise Point? That's one of my favorite places in the world!"

"*Jah*. Last summer I went to Serenity Ridge for the

first time for the annual fish fry and canoe race. Some of us hiked to Paradise Point after we ate."

At the end of every summer, the Amish community in Arleta's hometown had a tradition of hosting a big picnic and canoe race on Serenity Lake. They invited all the Amish people in Serenity Ridge, as well as those in Unity. Lately they'd begun to include the growing community in New Hope, too. The daylong event was so popular that the people who lived too far away to make the round-trip in one day by buggy either hired van drivers to take them to Serenity Ridge or else they stayed overnight with friends and relatives in the community, to give their horses a rest.

"Wait a second!" Arleta exclaimed. "Do you know the *mann* from New Hope who fell out of his canoe?"

"He didn't fall—he *jumped*. His *hut* blew off so he leaped in to get it."

"That's right—I'd forgotten. I didn't see it happen, but everyone thought he was a little *narrish*, since *hiet* are a dime a dozen and he got his clothes all wet. And his canoe was in the lead until then, if I remember correctly."

"*Jah*, but what people don't know is that he had secured the cash he'd brought to pay the van driver beneath the ribbon on his *hut*. That's why he jumped in after it."

"Oh, *neh*! Was the money still there when he fished the *hut* out?"

"*Neh*. Unfortunately, as soon as he hit the water, he remembered he'd been worried he'd lose the money and earlier that morning, he'd stuck it under a rock on shore. So he jumped in for nothing."

Arleta chuckled. That was the kind of harebrained thing one of her brothers would have done. "I never heard that part of the story."

"Nobody has—he only admitted it right now. You see, *I* was the *mann* who jumped overboard."

"That was *you*?" She stopped walking and clutched her sides, laughing.

"*Jah.* It was me." Isaiah grinned, too. "But please don't tell anyone the part about my money… I already feel *lecherich* enough that everyone in New Hope knows I was the one who jumped overboard to save my *hut*."

"I won't," she promised, glancing over her shoulder to see if Hannah and Noah were following closely enough to overhear their conversation.

They were several yards behind, but if they'd heard, it didn't register on their faces. In the brief glimpse she'd caught of them, Arleta noticed Hannah had her arms folded across her chest as she walked, and she was slightly ahead of Noah. They didn't seem to be enjoying themselves. Was she wrong? Were they interested in each other or weren't they? She couldn't help but wonder if they were and this was the first time Hannah had found out Arleta was staying with Noah and Sovilla. Maybe Hannah was annoyed that he hadn't told her before now.

That's pure conjecture, she told herself. *Just because Faith is obviously using this opportunity to spend time with Jacob doesn't mean that there's anything going on between Noah and Hannah*. Still, she didn't want to risk

Hannah getting the impression that there was anything going on between Arleta and Noah, either. So, she stuck close to Isaiah's side, chatting away.

"What's your vocation, Isaiah?" she questioned.

"I'm a *bauer*. My father owns a potato *bauerei*," he answered, which caused Arleta to burst out laughing. Isaiah stopped walking and stared at her, one eyebrow raised. "What's *voll schpass* about being a potato *bauer*?"

Clearly Arleta had offended him, and she felt so bad that she didn't stop to consider her response, answering honestly, "I wasn't laughing at your vocation, I promise. It's just that my little *schweschder* is convinced I'll meet a young potato *bauer* in New Hope and we'll start courting and I won't want to return to Serenity Ridge."

At first, Isaiah looked even more taken aback than when Arleta had laughed. But amusement danced across his face. "Is that so?" was all he said, but Arleta was mortified.

Me and my big moul! *He probably thinks I'm dropping a hint.* Her embarrassment was compounded when she realized Noah and Hannah had caught up with them and they must have heard what she'd said, too. She briefly considered adding that her sister often allowed her imagination to run away with her and the last thing Arleta wanted was a suitor, but she knew if she opened her mouth again, she'd only make matters worse. So, without another word, she silently started walking again, trying to look on the bright side. *At least if Hannah heard me, she'll think I'm interested in Isaiah, not in Noah...*

* * *

As the foursome silently trudged along the path that descended toward the floor of the gorge, Noah almost wished he could have spent the afternoon with Honor. Even chipping a tooth on one of her rock-hard cookies would have been preferable to the uncomfortable silence between him and Hannah. The longer it went on, the more difficult it became to break, so instead of forcing small talk with her, he strained his ears to catch snippets of the conversation between Isaiah and Arleta. Judging from their laughter, the two of them were enjoying each other's company.

But he was surprised to overhear Arleta mention that her sister thought she'd meet a potato farmer to court. Even if she wasn't aware that anyone except Isaiah could hear her, it was a very forward remark for an Amish woman to make to a man. However, Isaiah didn't appear to be at all fazed or put off by her boldness. On the contrary, there was a spring in his step as he walked side by side with her to the bottom of the gorge, where Jacob and Faith were splashing each other in the narrow and shallow but quick-moving stream.

"You took so long that we were concerned you'd lost your way," Faith said.

"You weren't concerned enough to *kumme* look for us," Hannah pointed out.

It was the first thing she'd said during their entire hike. Clearly she wasn't fooled by Faith's remark—it must have been clear to everyone by now that Faith and Jacob had deliberately rushed ahead so they could be alone. Not that Hannah or Noah were in any position to judge. They had done the same kind of thing when they were courting, even if they were more discreet about it.

"*Neh*, but we did wait for you," Faith replied.

"But we're not going to wait much longer—I'm *hungerich*," Jacob complained. "Everybody needs to take off your shoes and socks so we can cross the stream to pick up the trail on the other side."

"Why do we have to cross here? Isn't there some place drier we can walk?" Arleta asked.

"*Neh*. Usually, this *is* the driest spot to cross, but we've had a lot more rain than usual this spring. It doesn't get very deep. Up to your knees at most."

Arleta scrunched up her face. "I'm the shortest one here. The water might get up to *your* knees, but it will be much deeper on me. I'm going to turn around and walk back the way I came."

"That will take forever," Faith warned her. "This is a shortcut. The parking lot is only about ten minutes from here once we cross the stream."

Arleta insisted, "That's okay. I don't mind walking. I'll meet you back there—you don't have to wait for me to start lunch. I brought fried *hinkel*. Noah can get the cooler from the buggy."

It would take a good hour and a half for Arleta to return, and Noah didn't want to wait that long for her to get back. His hope was that they could gobble down their supper and then he and Arleta could be on their way. Besides, since this was Arleta's first time on the trail, she might get lost if she hiked back alone. Noah didn't want to loop back with her, but she was his employee, which in a way made her his responsibility. So he tried to convince her she'd be perfectly safe crossing the stream.

"There are five of us here. We're not going to let you slip and go under, if that's what you're worried about."

"It isn't," she said. "I—I—I just don't want to get my feet and legs wet. I'll get too cold."

"It's not as if it's the middle of winter," Noah argued. If he wasn't mistaken, her forehead was perspiring, so why was she being so unreasonable?

Isaiah, who had already removed his socks and shoes, offered, "I can carry you across, Arleta."

"Oh, *neh*! I can't let you do that," she protested.

"Sure, you can," he countered. "It will be better than walking all the way back, won't it?"

Arleta bit her lip and glanced at the stream. Noah couldn't tell if she was being coquettish—for all he knew, getting Isaiah to carry her had been her plan all along—or if she earnestly was wary about him picking her up. "Oh…okay," she agreed.

Isaiah leaned down and instructed her, "Take hold of my neck." After she did, he wrapped one arm around her back and supported her lower body with the other arm. By this time, Jacob and Faith had already crossed over to the other side and Hannah was midway there. "Grab my shoes and socks, will you?" he called to Noah.

Get them yourself, Noah thought, but he picked the footwear off the rock where Isaiah had set it. He felt irrationally irritated as he watched the strong, tall farmer gently placing Arleta on the embankment on the opposite side of the stream, and when he heard her thank him profusely in return. It made them seem as if they were enamored with each other.

Am I envious? he asked himself. He didn't think so; it wasn't as if *he* were enamored with Arleta. But if she and Isaiah were going to start up a courtship, Noah wished he didn't have to bear witness to it. Just like he wished he wasn't going to have to listen to Jacob carry on about his budding romance with Faith at work the following week. Watching other young people develop relationships with each other didn't make Noah jealous; it made him *sad.* Because it reminded him of the family he'd lost and the family he'd never have.

But that certainly wasn't Arleta's and Isaiah's or Faith's and Jacob's fault. And Noah couldn't hold it against Hannah, either. The night of the fire, she'd kept telling him it was late and he ought to get back home. He was the one who wanted to stay a little longer. To kiss her a little longer… Now, he could hardly stand to look at her because of the regretful memories he experienced when he did. Not that she ever gave him a second look, either. He had broken off their courtship before his family was even buried. And when he did, she hadn't cried, hadn't protested; she'd just remained silent and averted her eyes—just as she'd done while they were hiking—as if she wished he'd disappear…

Recalling that period in his life always made Noah feel glum. After everyone had put their shoes and socks back on again and hurried toward the parking lot, exuberantly discussing the supper they were about to enjoy, he dallied behind them. They took their coolers from the buggies and found a picnic table beneath the pine trees. Fortunately, he was able to sit at the opposite end of the bench from Hannah.

Noah felt so morose by then that he could hardly taste his food, but Isaiah, who was sitting next to him, remarked, "This is the most *appenditlich* potato salad I've ever eaten. And trust me, I know my potatoes. Who made it?"

"I did," Arleta said. "I'm *hallich* you like it."

"Apparently that's not all he likes," Jacob uttered just loud enough for Noah to hear him. "I told you there would be other *manner* interested in courting her. Looks like you lost your chance."

"Absatz," Noah warned him in an equally low voice. "I mean it. Knock it off."

Jacob just chuckled. "Somebody's a sore loser."

Everyone was so hungry from the long hike that they quickly devoured their meal before diving into Arleta's whoopie pies and the bumbleberry pie Hannah had made for dessert.

"Mmm, this is yummy. I can taste that it has strawberries, raspberries, blueberries and… What's the tart taste?"

"Rhubarb," Hannah answered Arleta. "I'd frozen the rest of the fruit from last year's crop, but the rhubarb is fresh from the garden."

"It's amazingly *gut*. Bumbleberry is Noah's *groossmammi*'s favorite kind of pie. I've never made one before but I'd really like to. Did you use a special recipe?"

"Jah—it's actually Sovilla's. She's the one who taught me how to make this kind of pie in the first place," Hannah replied.

Noah caught his breath, remembering. Hannah hadn't grown up in New Hope; she had moved there when she was about sixteen. Noah's sister, Mary, became fast friends with her and one day, Sovilla offered to disclose her secret ingredient. Noah had been hanging around the kitchen, threatening to listen in unless they promised to give him the biggest slice when the pie was done baking.

That was when he first developed an interest in Hannah, but as he recalled that afternoon now, he didn't remember as much about her as he remembered about his sister. Specifically, that she had literally swept him out the door with a broom! As the only girl in the family, she'd always struggled to keep the boys from intruding on what she considered to be her territory, which included time with her friends. But even when she became annoyed, Noah always felt her affection toward him and he hoped she'd always known how much he loved her, too, despite his teasing.

"I'll ask her for it, then," Arleta suggested. "Maybe one day when her immune system is stronger and the berries are ripe, you could *kumme* over and we could bake a couple of pies together."

Noah felt his stomach twist; but fortunately, Hannah declined, saying, "I don't know when I'd get the time—my *familye* is preparing to open a restaurant and we expect to be very busy, especially once the vacationers arrive for the summer. But I'm sure Sovilla could talk you through the steps, even if she couldn't show you."

Noah breathed a sigh of relief; Hannah seemed to be as averse to the idea of coming to his house as he was to the idea of having her there.

* * *

Arleta noticed the brusqueness in Hannah's tone right away. Everyone else in the group had been friendly, but Hannah had hardly spoken a word to her. Was she just a reserved person or was it possible she really was interested in Noah and the two of them were at odds for some reason? They'd seemed absolutely miserable walking together, as if they'd had a spat. Whatever it was about, Hannah couldn't have possibly thought Arleta was interested in Noah after she'd allowed Isaiah to carry her across the stream, could she?

As embarrassed as she'd been by Isaiah's offer and as much as she feared she might have misled him to believe she was flirting with him, Arleta was deeply grateful he'd saved her from having to remove her shoes and socks. She resented it that even a simple thing like going on a hike could potentially result in her secret being revealed. This wasn't like being home, where she knew everyone and every place and she could anticipate situations that might lead to someone discovering her tattoo. Arleta realized that she'd be better off not going hiking again rather than to risk another close call like the one she'd experienced at the edge of the stream.

"If you're done eating, I think we should leave now, Arleta," Noah suggested.

"Why are you running off so soon?" Jacob groused. "We're planning to go to the pond on the other side of the woods."

"*Jah.* Stay a little longer," Faith pleaded.

Arleta sensed the young woman was concerned that if they left, the others might want to go home, too, which would mean her time with Jacob would come to an end for the day. But Arleta was spent, both emotionally and physically, so she replied, "We told Sovilla we wouldn't be gone very long. But it was a lot of *schpass* to meet everyone. *Denki* for inviting me and showing me the gorge."

"I hope we see you again soon, Arleta," Isaiah said. Then, as almost an afterthought he added, "You, too, Noah. It's nice to spend time with you outside of *kurrich*."

Noah responded with curt goodbyes, and Arleta followed him to the buggy. He was quiet as they headed home, and she wondered if he was upset about whatever was possibly going on between him and Hannah. Regardless of the reason, Arleta got the distinct feeling he regretted going hiking. Sovilla must have noticed his expression when they arrived home, too. After Lovina left and while Noah was out in the barn doing the second milking, she asked Arleta if something upsetting had happened during the hike.

"*N-neh*, nothing in particular," she hedged, reluctant to confide her observation about Hannah and Noah to Sovilla.

Sovilla pressed. "In general, then?"

"*Neh*, in general, we had a nice time," Arleta answered truthfully. Then she quickly redirected the conversation. "The gorge is beautiful—I've never seen anything like it. And Hannah Miller made the most *appenditlich* bumbleberry pie I've ever tasted. She said she used your special recipe. I'd love to make it for you as soon as the berries are ripe for picking."

"Hannah Miller went on the hike?"

Ach. When will I learn that silence is golden? Arleta reluctantly answered, *"Jah."*

"Ah, that would explain it." Sovilla nodded, as if everything made sense.

Now it was Arleta's turn to dig for information. "Explain what?"

"Noah's mood." Sovilla leaned forward. "I probably shouldn't tell you this, but I can trust you not to let on you know, can't I?"

Arleta's curiosity to know what had happened between Hannah and Noah outweighed her guilt about gossiping about them. She nodded. "I won't say a word to anyone."

"I suspect Noah doesn't even know I'm aware of this, but he used to be Hannah's suitor. She was the only *maedel* he courted, as far as I know—and I'm usually right." She adjusted the kerchief on her head and glanced toward the door. "After the fire, he broke it off with her, though. I think he felt like his primary responsibility was to take care of *me*."

Arleta allowed herself a moment to absorb this information. Although she felt a small measure of satisfaction in knowing that she hadn't just imagined the tension between Hannah and Noah, she realized she hadn't exactly interpreted the situation correctly. "And you think she's still upset about him ending their courtship? Or that *he's* still upset about ending it?"

Sovilla shook her head. "What I think might be more likely is that Noah could feel… Well, I suspect being around her might make him realize he passed up the opportunity to get married and start a *familye*. Most of the time I think he's able to suppress those feelings, but whenever he sees Hannah, he has to face the life he could have had. Even catching a glimpse of her at *kurrich* seems to put him in a sour mood."

"But he's so young. He can *still* have a wife and *kinner*," Arleta said. *It's not as if he has a tattoo on his ankle and a regrettable past.*

Sovilla sighed, her eyes brimming. "That's what I tell him, but he won't listen. I'm afraid that until I go home to be with the Lord, he's not going to even consider courting anyone. It troubles me deeply to know I'm the reason he isn't pursuing a romantic relationship…"

"That's nonsense!" Arleta was appalled that Sovilla would say such a thing, which seemed akin to suggesting she'd have to die in order for Noah to be happy. "There's no reason he can't start courting someone right now. In fact, there's no reason he—"

She was going to say, "There's no reason he can't court Hannah Miller again if he wants to, provided she'd be willing to give their relationship another try," but Sovilla lifted a finger to her lips as the kitchen door opened. So Arleta excused herself to go to her room, just as Noah came in. She pulled out her stationery to begin her second letter to her sister that week, but instead of writing, she stared out the window, chewing on the tip of her pen. She thought about how remorseful Sovilla seemed to be that her grandson was apparently putting his responsibility toward her above seeking a relationship that might eventually lead to marriage.

How can I encourage Noah to resume his courtship

with Hannah? she wondered. *I'm sure that once she spends a little time around him again, she'll remember what a considerate, kind and responsible man he is. And with a little encouragement, he'll realize that there's no reason he can't be a suitor* and *a dutiful grandson.*

Arleta considered enlisting Sovilla's help in getting them together, but she instantly realized that plan could easily backfire, as Noah would suspect his grandmother was trying to play matchmaker. Then it occurred to Arleta that she was becoming something of a meddlesome matchmaker herself. So she focused on writing a letter to her sister instead. In it, she described the trip she'd taken to the gorge, briefly mentioning that a potato farmer had carried her across the stream. *But don't worry*, she scrawled, *I have no romantic interest in him whatsoever.*

Then, without registering what she was doing, she added, *If I were to become interested in anyone romantically, it would be Noah, not Isaiah.* When she reread the paragraph, Arleta clapped her hand over her mouth. How had that thought crept into her mind and onto the page? Chagrinned, she scribbled it out as quickly as she could and blotted it from her mind, as well.

"Did you have a nice time hiking with your friends?" Sovilla asked Noah when he sat down in the armchair opposite the sofa.

"It was fine."

"Arleta told me Hannah Miller went."

So that was what the two of them were whispering about when I came in. Aware his grandmother was gauging his reaction, Noah responded nonchalantly, "*Jah*, Hannah was there. As well as Faith, Jacob and Isaiah."

"Isaiah Wittmer? Arleta didn't mention he was there, too."

"I'm not surprised," he muttered.

"Why? Didn't the two of them get along?"

"Oh, they got along all right…he carried her across a stream." As soon as the words were out of Noah's mouth, he realized that in an effort to distract his grandmother from drilling him about Hannah, he'd sacrificed Arleta's privacy. He felt a twinge of guilt, knowing his grandmother would ask her all sorts of nosy questions she'd be too polite not to answer. *That's not really my fault*, he tried to assure himself. *If she didn't want anyone commenting on her behavior, she shouldn't have been so finicky about crossing the stream like everyone else.*

"Why would he do something like that?"

Because he likes *her, obviously.* Noah was surprised his grandmother didn't leap to this conclusion herself, but he was too embarrassed to spell it out for her. "She was afraid to cross it and she wanted to turn around and walk all the way back the way we came."

"Then why didn't *you* help her?" Sovilla asked. She was giving him the same look she'd given him when he'd asked Arleta if her socks were clean. "I can understand if you didn't want to carry her across yourself, but you should have at least walked back with her if that's what made her feel more comfortable. You ought to be more responsible, Noah. She's our guest."

Neh, *she's our employee*, he silently argued. "Isaiah seemed eager to carry her and Arleta didn't appear to mind, either."

Sovilla exhaled heavily, her shoulders drooping. "I warned you to keep an eye out for her, didn't I?"

"But, *Groossmammi*, nothing happened. She's fine. She didn't so much as get her toes wet."

"*Jah*, thanks to Isaiah Wittmer."

That's when Noah finally caught on: his grandmother didn't want Isaiah to take an interest in Arleta. *I think it may be too late for that. But why would she care anyway?* Was it because she was harboring a hope that *Noah* would want to court Arleta? *If that's what she's thinking, then* Groossmammi *is bound to be disappointed, because I'm not any more likely to become Arleta's suitor than I am to start courting Hannah Miller again.*

He was about to say something to that effect, but his grandmother looked so crestfallen already that he didn't want to upset her further. So instead, he offered to fix her a cup of tea. Then, the two of them chatted and played a couple of games of checkers, which was how he wished he'd spent the afternoon in the first place.

Chapter Five

In the weeks following the outing to the gorge, Arleta noticed a small but definite improvement in Sovilla's energy level. She was still taking naps a couple of times a day, but they were getting shorter and she was able to stroll to the end of the lane daily, arm in arm with Arleta to pick up the mail. Her appetite was improving, too, which made Arleta happy since she'd checked several cookbooks out of the library to supplement the recipes she'd been using from Sovilla's recipe box in an attempt to prepare a wider variety of healthy meals.

Although Sovilla had two more months to wait before being retested for cancer, she saw her local doctor for a routine visit and the doctor was extremely pleased with the improvements in her overall recovery so far. She cautioned Sovilla to continue avoiding anyone who was ill and to keep wearing a mask while attending large gatherings, like church. But she lifted the restriction on visiting households with small children, which was the majority of Amish families in New Hope.

"Let's stop at the Bawells' *haus*," Sovilla excitedly suggested on the way home. "Lovina's been praying faithfully for me and I want to tell her the *gut* news."

Arleta hesitated. "It's almost four o'clock. Don't you think we should go straight home so I can prepare supper?"

"There's no rush. We had a late lunch, and Noah hasn't been getting home until almost seven thirty or eight o'clock."

It was true; he had developed a routine of going from working with his crew directly to working on extra individual projects by himself. Arleta usually packed him enough food to last through the day. Depending on what time he came home and whether he was hungry still, in the evenings she'd warm up leftovers of whatever supper she'd made for Sovilla and herself.

But since he'd gotten a ride from Mike today so Arleta could use the buggy to take Sovilla to her appointment, she knew he'd have to be dropped off at home to take the buggy to his second worksite. She figured he'd probably want a quick supper before he left again. But Arleta didn't want to dampen Sovilla's joyfulness, so she redirected the horse toward Lovina's house for a brief visit.

As they turned into the dirt driveway, they spotted Lovina's grandchildren rolling down a small hill on the side of the house. It reminded Arleta of when she was young, and it made her miss her family. Although she enjoyed being with Sovilla and felt she was overpaid to do such light work, Arleta still was having difficulty adjusting to being so isolated. *Maybe now that Sovilla*

*is stronger, Noah will relax a little and we can have
company more frequently,* she thought.

"Look at how *schnuck* they are," Sovilla remarked
with a sigh. "I wonder if the Lord will ever bless me
with *kinskinner.*"

Not if Noah keeps up the same work schedule, Arleta thought, pulling up beside the hitching post by the
Bawells' barn. After the hike to the gorge, she'd hoped
her presence with Sovilla might free Noah up to do a
little more socializing on the weekends—especially
with Hannah. But he worked from eight o'clock in the
morning until almost eight at night on Saturdays. And
he was usually so tired from putting in such long hours
during the week that all he wanted to do after worship
services on Sunday was take a nap and play an occasional game of spades. *At this rate, Lovina's kinskinner
will be courting before Noah is,* Arleta mused.

"Sovilla and Arleta, what a *wunderbaar* surprise,"
Lovina exclaimed a few minutes later when they came
up the walkway. She'd been sweeping the porch but she
set aside her broom to welcome them as Arleta assisted
Sovilla up the steps. After taking a seat in the wooden
glider, Sovilla told Lovina what the doctor had said
about her health. Lovina tucked her chin to her chest
and thanked the Lord aloud before settling onto the
bench beside her friend.

Just then, three young women came out of the house.
Arleta knew Hannah Miller and she'd met Lovina's
daughter-in-law, Ruth, at church. The third woman introduced herself as Ruth's daughter Honor, who had
been out of town for several weeks. She poured every-

one a glass of meadow tea—a sweetened, chilled drink made from water and brewed mint—with lemon slices.

The young women were gleeful to hear about the improvement in Sovilla's health. In turn, she asked after Hannah's parents—her mother was ill—and Ruth's children before the conversation turned to gardening and canning. Hannah mentioned what a plentiful rhubarb crop her family had that spring, adding, "It's *gut* that we've harvested most of it already, since it doesn't thrive in hot weather."

"*I* don't thrive in hot weather, either." Honor fanned her face with her hand. "I don't know how you can stand to wear stockings and shoes, Arleta."

Arleta quickly scanned the other women's feet, realizing none of them was wearing shoes except for Sovilla, and hers were slide-on sandals. "I'm really used to them, so they don't bother me," she answered honestly. Then she quickly changed the subject, asking Honor about her visit to her sister and brother-in-law's house in Ohio.

Honor explained that her eldest sister, Eve, was almost fifteen years older than she was and she'd just delivered her sixth child, so she needed additional help running her household. "My niece Katie is sixteen now so she's finished with *schul*, but she's working out as a nanny, so she's not able to help my *schweschder* with her littler ones."

Lovina clucked her tongue and abashedly explained to the other women, "I know what you're thinking—it's a shame that Katie is taking care of an *Englischer*'s *kinner* instead of helping her *mamm* by watching her own *brieder* and *schweschdere*. Unfortunately, after last year's setback with the barley crop, money is tight in their *familye*. And there aren't many opportunities for *meed* to earn an income where my *dochder* lives. Still, I told Eve she may regret allowing her *dochder* to be yoked to an *Englisch* employer, especially because she's still on *rumspringa* and hasn't been baptized into the *kurrich* yet. The temptations of the world can be overwhelming to deny, especially when a young person comes into contact with them every day."

"*Gott* willing, the *maedel* will hold fast to her up-bringing," Sovilla said, comforting her. "Arleta worked out when she was on her *rumspringa*, and she didn't stray from her faith."

Heat rose in Arleta's face. One day when she'd been cleaning the windows, she offhandedly let it slip to Sovilla that her *Englisch* employer had wanted her to use an expensive "green" cleaning solution on the sliding glass doors, but Arleta thought hot water and vinegar were even more effective. They'd had a brief discussion about Arleta's role as the Fairfaxes' housekeeper, but she wished Sovilla hadn't mentioned it in front of the other women, since most Amish people she knew didn't look favorably on Amish youth working out. And she especially wished Sovilla hadn't used her as an example of someone who had been faithful to her Amish beliefs. *If she only knew what I was really like and what I'd been close to doing, she wouldn't be so quick to soothe Lovina's qualms*, she thought.

"When I was at Eve's *haus*, I heard Katie tell her younger *schweschdere* about a handheld vacuum cleaner she used to clean up after the *Englisch kinner* made a mess with crackers," Honor confided in disgust. "It's a shame how she's filling their minds with images of conveniences that might make them envious of the *Englisch* lifestyle."

As the other women expressed their disapproval, Arleta looked intently at the glass she held on her lap. Whoever had made the tea hadn't strained it properly and the drink was speckled with mint leaves. She focused on the little flecks to keep herself from tearing up. She understood why the women were critical of allowing a sixteen-year-old girl to work full-time in an *Englischer*'s home. And she would certainly do her best to dissuade her parents from ever allowing Leanna to work in an *Englischer*'s house if the possibility arose in the future. But a little part of her wanted to ask, *Even if you haven't been tempted by the* Englisch *lifestyle, haven't any of you ever made choices or done things in violation of your faith? Or am I the only one?*

"Arleta?" Sovilla interrupted her thoughts. All eyes were on her. "Ruth asked if you want more tea."

"*Denki*, but no," she replied. "I'm sorry. I was just thinking of my little *schweschder*, Leanna."

"You must miss her," Honor said. "You ought to *kumme* to our work frolic tomorrow morning. Tell her about it, Hannah."

Hannah hesitated before explaining, "Because my *mamm* has been ill, I need help cleaning the restaurant before my *brieder* can move the new tables and chairs in. The last owners left the place in a mess. Honor said she'd help and Faith Smoker will be there, too."

Hannah's comments weren't exactly an invitation to participate. Not that it mattered, since Arleta couldn't leave Sovilla alone for that long, anyway. But it stung a little that she didn't even ask; she hadn't seemed any friendlier toward Arleta today than she had the day they went hiking. Arleta sipped her tea and then discreetly pinched a piece of mint from her tongue and wiped her fingers on her apron.

"You should *kumme*, Arleta," Honor repeated. "Jacob and Isaiah are going to be there helping Hannah's *breider* repaint the walls. Instead of bringing our lunches, we're ordering pizza and I'm bringing peach *kuchen* for dessert."

Sovilla echoed, "*Jah*, you should go, Arleta."

"I'd like to, but Noah won't be home," she protested, knowing he'd object to his grandmother being left alone for the day. To the others, she explained, "He's trying to catch up with a backlog of customers, so he's been working on *Samschdaag* lately."

"All the more reason to go," Sovilla insisted. "You need to get out and enjoy being with your friends, and I need to stay in and enjoy being by myself."

Even though she knew the older woman hadn't intended to hurt her feelings, Arleta's eyes smarted. "I'd be *hallich* to help," she said feebly to Hannah.

"*Gut.* I'd appreciate it," the young woman replied, although Arleta couldn't help but think her pinched expression told a different story.

It had been a long day, and every muscle in Noah's body ached. The crew had been putting in even longer hours than usual this week because they were coming up on a deadline, and Jacob had been out sick on Monday and Tuesday. Ordinarily, Noah would have been concerned about catching Jacob's illness and bringing it home to his grandmother, but he doubted the teenager was truly sick. Instead, he guessed he was run-down from courting Faith on the weekends. Although Noah's parents had been strict about his curfew, he knew many Amish youth who stayed out until one or two o'clock on Saturday and Sunday evenings when they were courting. It seemed unlikely that Jacob's aunts would have imposed a curfew on him, so as the men were dispersing on Friday afternoon, Noah casually remarked, "I hope you're not going to stay out too late this weekend, Jacob."

"It depends on how much *schpass* I'm having," the teenager replied, grinning. Clearly, he wasn't taking the hint seriously, so Noah tried again.

"You have a responsibility to your crew, and we all have a responsibility to our customers," he reminded him. "It's important we honor *Gott* and demonstrate our beliefs to the *Englisch* by working hard and keeping our commitments."

"It's also important we honor *Gott* and demonstrate our beliefs by not valuing earning money above spending time with our *familye* and community," Jacob countered.

Noah immediately understood what he was implying. *It might look like I'm motivated by greed, but he has no idea why I'm trying to earn money. It's for my* familye, he rationalized as he rode home with Mike in silence.

He suspected that Jacob was just trying to distract him from the teenager's own behavior, but the comment still troubled him. Did Noah's district see him the same way Jacob did? Did the *Englisch* community see him that way, too? He was tempted to ask Mike his opinion, but he decided against it. *The Lord knows the intentions of my heart. He's the only one I need to please.*

It was a little after six o'clock when his coworker dropped him off. Hungry for supper and eager to hear what the doctor had said, he briskly strode into the house, but he found it empty. Arleta and Sovilla definitely should have been home by now. His first thought was that the doctor had noticed something alarming in regard to his grandmother's health and she'd been sent to the hospital. He immediately bowed his head and asked the Lord to protect and heal her—but even before he opened his eyes, he heard the clip-clopping of the horse's hooves coming up the lane.

"*Groossmammi*, are you okay?" he asked after he'd rushed outside to the buggy to help her down.

"I'm *gut*. I'll tell you all about it as soon as we're inside." Sovilla took hold of his arm for balance, but Noah had been so concerned something was wrong with her that *his* legs felt shaky as they made their way to the door.

While he was thrilled when his grandmother said the doctor was encouraged by her progress, he was less than happy that Sovilla had celebrated by socializing with several women from different households all at once. He wished Arleta had exercised better judgment than to bring her to a gathering the very afternoon she'd received an encouraging health report. He hoped she wasn't going to abandon all of the guidelines he'd made concerning his grandmother's well-being.

His displeasure must have shown on his face because Sovilla quickly added, "We only intended to stay for a few minutes, but it felt so *normal* to sit out on the porch, visiting with a group of *weibsleit* again that I didn't want to leave. Poor Arleta practically had to drag me away—she wanted to get home to cook your supper."

"That would have been nice, but I don't have time to wait until it's prepared." Noah directed his comment to Arleta, who was rushing around the kitchen, washing vegetables and pulling pots from the cupboard.

"It will only take a few minutes," she blithely assured him. "Besides, where's the fire?"

Although he knew it was only a figure of speech meaning *what's the hurry*, Noah felt his stomach cramp into a knot and his appetite completely left him. He nervously muttered, "I—I have to finish installing a roof for a *familye* over at the Grandview Estates. If you can believe it, it's for their *dochder*'s playhouse."

"Oh, I can believe the *Englisch* would spend that kind of money on a roof for their *dochder*'s *haus*," Sovilla said. "But what I can't believe is that you'd rush off to install it for them instead of enjoying one of Arleta's *appenditlich* meals with us. This is a time for rejoicing together, isn't it?"

"*Jah*, you're right, it is," Noah begrudgingly agreed. Even though he no longer felt like eating, he supposed he could spare a few minutes—and spare himself an argument with his grandmother—to sit down to supper with them.

Fortunately, Arleta fixed a light meal that was comprised almost exclusively of vegetables. After giving thanks for the food, as well as for his grandmother's improved health, Noah stuck his fork into a spear of asparagus and lifted it to his mouth. It was unusually tender; his grandmother's steamed asparagus was always so reedy he felt like a cow chewing its cud whenever he ate it, but Arleta had gotten this just right. He could feel his appetite kicking in again, and he downed his meal quickly before rising to leave.

He was halfway to the Grandview Estates when a loud crack of thunder sounded overhead, followed by a brilliant sequence of lightning. He turned around and managed to get the horse into the stable, unhitch the buggy and make it to the porch before the sky let loose a torrential downpour.

"Sovilla went to bed already. I think she was worn out from all the excitement about what her *dokder* said," Arleta told him when he came into the kitchen where she was drying the last of the supper dishes.

"*Jah*. And from all the gallivanting around. Tomorrow it might be better if she's not with so many people," he suggested pointedly as he untied his laces and slid his boots off.

"Don't worry. She wants to stay in alone. And I'll even be at a work frolic in the morning."

"You're leaving her by herself?"

"*Jah*. She said she'll be fine. I'll only be gone a few

hours—I don't intend to stay as long as everyone else does. I'll *kumme* home after lunch."

"Where is the frolic?"

"It's at the Millers' new restaurant. We'll be preparing it for opening day." Arleta stood on her tiptoes to put a plate into the cupboard. Over her shoulder, she said, "It's too bad you can't *kumme*. We're getting pizza delivered and Honor's making peach *kuchen*—although considering how you feel about her cooking, that might not be much of an enticement."

Noah wasn't in the mood for kidding around. *Why is Arleta going to a work frolic when she knows how I feel about* Groossmammi *being left alone?*

"I appreciate it that you want to socialize and contribute to the needs of our district, but I'm not paying you to help the Millers with their restaurant. I'm paying you to help my *groossmammi* during her recovery," he said.

Arleta closed the cupboard door and turned to face him. Her voice quavering, she replied, "Your *groossmammi* was the one who insisted I go to the work frolic. I tried to tell her I didn't think that was a *gut* idea, but she said she wanted time alone in the *haus*. If you'd prefer I don't go, that's fine with me. However, I'd appreciate it if you'd tell Sovilla why you want me to stay home, since I don't feel comfortable arguing with her about it." Arleta hung the dish towel on its hook and turned on her heel.

After she disappeared down the hallway, Noah plunked onto a chair with a groan. The only thing that ached more than his muscles was his head, and he rubbed his temples in big, slow circles with his palms.

I'm sorry if I hurt her feelings, but I'm not sorry I made myself clear, he thought. *Because even if it was at* Groossmammi's *request this time, I don't want Arleta to get any ideas that this can be a common occurrence in the future.*

Yet two hours later, when his conscience kept him from sleeping even though he was physically depleted, Noah had to admit to himself how rude—how *wrong*—he'd been to speak to Arleta like he had. *I know better than anyone how insistent* Groossmammi *can be*, he acknowledged. *It must be difficult for someone as forbearing as Arleta to resist her wishes when she wants to go somewhere—or when she wants* Arleta *to go somewhere.*

Noah was ashamed for acting as if Arleta didn't prioritize caring for Sovilla, when he knew full well how diligent she'd been about keeping the house as germ-free as possible and fixing healthy meals for her. *If it weren't for Arleta,* Groossmammi *may not have received such a* gut *report from her* dokder *today*, he told himself. *I need to apologize to her first thing tomorrow morning.*

But the next day she wasn't in the kitchen when he passed through it on his way to go outside to the barn. And by the time he came in from milking the cow, Sovilla was up, too, which meant he didn't have privacy to speak to Arleta alone.

"Guder mariye," he cheerfully greeted them as he removed his boots. "It looks like it might rain." Then, by way of telling Arleta he'd changed his mind about her

going to the work frolic, he said, "I can give you a ride to the Millers' restaurant on my way to work, Arleta."

In the instant when she briefly glanced his way, he noticed her eyes were red-rimmed. Had she been crying? "*Denki*, but we're not meeting until nine o'clock. I know you're probably eager to get going right away since you couldn't work last night."

It was true that he'd suffered a setback because of the thunderstorm, but apologizing to Arleta suddenly seemed a lot more important than finishing the playhouse before noon, which was his self-imposed deadline. "That's okay. I don't mind waiting. We can go whenever you're ready."

"What a treat—to have you linger over breakfast," his grandmother responded earnestly, although Arleta didn't look quite as pleased.

She seemed even more reserved when she got into the buggy and they started out toward the Millers' restaurant. As eager as Noah was to apologize, Arleta's quietness unnerved him, and he struggled to come up with the right words to express how much he regretted saying the things he'd said the previous evening.

However, about a mile down the road, she broke the silence by saying, "I want you to know that I understand why you don't think it's fair to pay me when I'm not spending time with your *groossmammi*. And I hope you'll deduct today's wages from my salary for the week."

"What?" Had Noah really come across as being *that* concerned about money? Then he remembered what he'd said about how he wasn't paying Arleta to help with the Millers' restaurant. He turned to look at her. She had twisted her head to the side, gazing out over the meadow to her right, so that he only could see her ear and a part of her cheek. "I didn't mean what I said last night the way it came out."

"*Neh*, it's okay. It makes sense that you shouldn't pay me if I'm not actually doing what you hired me to do," she said softly. "And it makes sense that the timing is probably right for you to hire a different caregiver, too."

"What?" Noah asked again, even more appalled than when Arleta suggested he reduce her pay for the week. "You want to leave?"

Arleta didn't *want* to leave, for several reasons. First, she'd grown very fond of Sovilla and Noah. But even if she hadn't liked them so much, she had made a commitment and she believed she ought to honor it. Second, she needed the money if she ever hoped to have her tattoo removed. However, she'd tossed and turned all night ruminating over Sovilla's and Noah's remarks. And in the wee hours of the morning she'd come to the decision that—as disappointing as it would be—if they wanted her to leave, she'd make her departure as easy and amicable for them as she could.

"Your *groossmammi* is tiring of me—that's why she wanted me to go to the frolic. She said she wanted to be alone. And if I'm not at the *haus*, I can't be of any help to her, which means you're wasting your money paying me," Arleta explained, to show she'd taken his perspective into consideration. "Besides, her health is improving now and you probably don't need someone here full time."

"Whoa!" Noah commanded the horse to stop on the shoulder of the road. He pushed his hat back and peered intently at Arleta. "I'm sorry that what I said last night didn't reflect the depth of my appreciation for all that you've done. But I consider your presence in our home to be a gift from *Gott*. It's invaluable. Please don't leave because of something *dumm* I said that I didn't mean. I was overly tired and irritated at—at one of my coworkers and…well, there's no excuse. Please just forgive me—and don't leave."

Hearing Noah's compliment made Arleta feel as if she'd just swallowed a cupful of sunshine; it filled her with warmth from her cheeks to her toes. But as much as she treasured his words, she doubted Sovilla felt the same way. "I've enjoyed being at your *haus*, too. But your *groossmammi*—"

"She said something she didn't mean, too. Or she didn't mean it the way you took it. If I know my *groossmammi* as well as I think I do, she felt like you should go out and socialize once in a while instead of staying with her all the time. But she knew you'd resist it if she said that, so she turned the tables and claimed she wanted the *haus* to herself for a while."

That thought *had* occurred to Arleta, too. "*Jah*, perhaps."

"I'm sure of it. I can talk to her about it when—"

"*Neh*, please don't. I don't want to turn a molehill into a mountain." Arleta realized she should have spoken with Noah before jumping to the conclusion that neither he nor Sovilla wanted her to stay. But she'd been so homesick yesterday, and she'd felt even more alone after she'd listened to the other women implying how disgraceful it was for a young woman to work out. Hannah's lukewarm invitation to the frolic contributed to her loneliness, too. So by the time Sovilla and Noah made their remarks, Arleta already felt as if no one truly wanted her around and she jumped to the conclusion they would have preferred to employ someone else. She felt too silly to explain all of that to Noah now, so she simply said, "I shouldn't have been so sensitive."

"*Neh*. My *groossmammi* and I shouldn't have been so *in*sensitive." Noah's chocolate-colored eyes conveyed the sincerity of his words. "It can't be easy trying to please both of us at the same time."

Arleta laughed. Since she couldn't deny it, she said, "It might not always be easy, but it's always interesting."

"Interesting enough to stay for the rest of the summer?"

"*Jah*, of course. I'm *hallich* you haven't changed your mind."

"About you leaving New Hope? *Neh!*" he exclaimed. "But I have changed my mind about you leaving my *groossmammi* alone on occasion. *Not* because I think she's tiring of you, but because I think she's right. You need a little time away from the *haus*—*and* from the two of us."

"*Neh*, that's not necess—"

"It *is* necessary. It will be *gut* for you. And as long as my *groossmammi* feels okay, it will be *gut* for her, too. She never had anyone stay with her before she was ill, so I think being alone on occasion will help her feel as if things are a little more normal again. Kind of like what she said about visiting with Lovina and the others yesterday. Okay?" He looked expectantly at Arleta.

She nodded. "Okay. *Denki*."

"You're *wilkom*." He clicked his tongue and lifted the reins, urging the horse back onto the road. Although he was directing his gaze forward, his profile creased with a grin as he asked, "So, are you really going to be brave enough to try Honor's *kuchen*?"

"I don't think so," Arleta admitted. "I nearly choked on her meadow tea yesterday."

"Too much sugar?"

"Too many mint leaves! I wasn't sure if I was drinking meadow tea or celery soup." She laughed and Noah did, too. "But her cooking aside, I really do like her. She's been very welcoming to me." *Unlike Hannah*, Arleta thought ruefully.

They pulled into the restaurant's driveway next to a hitched horse and buggy she didn't recognize. When she climbed down, she noticed Isaiah crossing the driveway in their direction. He gave them both a big smile. "I didn't know you two were coming to help today."

"Noah's not staying," Arleta explained. "He's got to go to work."

"Cleaning and painting a restaurant isn't work?"

"*Neh*, I meant he's got to work for money. Not for *schpass*."

"I'm supposed to be working on the farm today, too, but I convinced my *daed* that it's more important that I give my friends a hand this morning," Isaiah said. Then he joked, "After all, the potatoes will still be there this afternoon—but the pizza won't still be *here*."

As Arleta chuckled, Noah unexpectedly volunteered, "I might *kumme* back later to help out, too."

Aware that the frolic might be the perfect opportunity for Noah to renew his romance with Hannah, Arleta knew she should encourage him to return. But instead she heard herself saying, "Don't trouble yourself, Noah. Everyone knows you've got a lot of customers to serve. The Millers have plenty of people here to help already. We'll be fine."

Noah tried not to feel affronted by Arleta's comment, but as he headed toward Grandview Estates, he brooded over what she meant by, "Everyone knows you've got a lot of customers to serve." *Is she implying that everyone thinks I've been serving the* Englisch *instead of serving* Gott *and my* kurrich? he wondered. But that didn't seem like something she'd say; *Jacob* might, but Arleta wouldn't. Maybe she just didn't want him to feel guilty if he couldn't return later to help because he got too caught up in whatever project he was working on.

Then another thought occurred to him: maybe she didn't *want* him to return later to help. If that was the case, he had a pretty good idea of what the reason was— she wanted to spend time with Isaiah without Noah noticing they were romantically interested in each other. Which would have been hard to miss since Isaiah had practically tripped over his own feet crossing the parking lot to greet her. But even if that wasn't the reason—even if she just wanted to be on her own with her peer group for a while—Noah knew it wasn't any of his business.

All that matters is that Arleta and I are on gut *terms with each other again and that she has no intention of leaving,* he told himself. *I encouraged her to take time away from* Groossmammi *and me and now I need to let her do just that.*

But the harder he tried to put the matter out of his mind, the more he thought about it. When he'd told Arleta she should feel free to get away to socialize on occasion, he'd envisioned her participating in a work frolic with her female friends. Or a quilting bee. A sister day. He hadn't imagined she'd be hanging out and eating pizza with Isaiah.

For the first time since…well, the first time in years, Noah wished *he* could be hanging out and eating pizza with other single people around his age, too, instead of working alone. In fact, his desire to be with his peer group—with Arleta in particular—even outweighed his awkwardness at seeing Hannah again. So when another thunderstorm broke out shortly after noon, forcing him to postpone completing the installation a second time, he decided he'd go lend a hand at the Millers' restaurant.

When he entered the building some twenty minutes later, Noah spotted Faith, Honor and Hannah mopping up the floor while Hannah's brothers were both standing on chairs by the window, apparently trying to manage a leak in the roof. Unsurprisingly to Noah, Jacob was sitting on a tabletop, swinging his legs and eating a slice of pizza. "What are you doing here?" he asked after Noah greeted everyone.

"I came to help. I can't stay too long because I don't want to leave my *groossmammi* alone all day, but I can put in a couple of hours of work," he offered. "Where's Arleta?"

"She got a ride home with Isaiah. You just missed her."

"But you're just in time to help us repair this wall," one of Hannah's brothers said. "Have a slice of pizza and then grab your toolbox and any roofing materials you have in your buggy."

"Sorry," Jacob mumbled, his mouth full. "This was the last piece. But there's plenty of *kuchen* left. Have some of that." He shot Noah a mischievous look.

"*Jah*, you can have a really big slice. I'll cut it for you," Honor offered, wiping her hands on her apron and walking over to serve him pie.

Deep down, Noah knew his primary intention in coming there wasn't to help—it was to interfere with Arleta and Isaiah becoming too friendly with each other. So when Honor handed him a plate, he thanked her and accepted what was probably an unsavory confection, figuring he was getting exactly what he deserved.

Chapter Six

When Isaiah dropped her off half an hour earlier, Arleta had discovered Sovilla asleep on the sofa. But now, as she passed through the living room with a basket of wet laundry that she hadn't been able to remove from the clothesline until the rain let up a little, the older woman's eyes fluttered open.

"Hi, Sovilla. Are you feeling okay?"

Sovilla adjusted her headscarf and pushed herself into an upright position. "I'm fine. I didn't plan on dozing off, though. *Kumme*, sit down and tell me all about your morning."

"I will, just as soon as I hang these clothes in the basement," Arleta replied.

"*Gut.* I'll fix us a cup of tea."

As Arleta wrung out the clothes and placed the wet dresses on hangers and clipped the socks, shirts and trousers to the rope strung in the basement, two things occurred to her. The first was that when she arrived here, Sovilla didn't have the strength to perform a simple task such as putting a kettle on for tea, like she did now. It was another small but important change. The *Englisch* doctor had looked at blood counts and X-rays to determine how well she was recovering, but Arleta was more impressed that she could now navigate around her kitchen unassisted again—an especially significant milestone for an Amish woman. Sovilla might not have been able to prepare meals quite yet, but she seemed well on her way.

The second thing that struck her was how eager Sovilla seemed to chat with her, which made Arleta wonder if she'd only been napping to pass the time while she was alone. *I hope she wasn't too restless*, Arleta thought.

In any case, nothing about her demeanor now indicated that she'd been *glad* to get rid of Arleta for a few hours. Quite the opposite; she seemed glad to have her home again. *I don't know how I could have thought she was tiring of me—at least not to the point of wanting me to leave permanently*, Arleta mused once again. Furthermore, she recognized that even if Sovilla *had* needed a little time to herself, she shouldn't have taken it personally. After all, Arleta felt better for having gotten out of the house, too, just as Noah had implied would be the case. She hurried upstairs to tell Sovilla all about the work frolic, including who was there, what they did and what the restaurant looked like inside.

"So did Honor give you a ride home or did Faith?"

"Actually, neither of them did. Isaiah brought me home, since he had work he needed to do on the farm."

"In the rain?" Sovilla raised an eyebrow.

Nothing gets past her. Arleta had also been leery of Isaiah's claim that he was needed on the farm—or at least, that he had urgent work to do in the fields. She suspected the same thing Sovilla clearly did: that he'd been making up an excuse because he wanted to be alone with Arleta. Ordinarily she would have declined the ride and waited until the skies cleared before she walked home, since she didn't want to give him the impression that she reciprocated his interest. But to be honest, she was eager to get back.

For one thing, she was growing wary of Hannah's distinct unfriendliness toward her. She didn't treat anyone else that way. While Arleta appreciated that Hannah didn't know her nearly as well as she knew the others, she thought that should have been all the more reason for Hannah to be inclusive toward her. If the shoe were on the other foot and Hannah were the newcomer, Arleta would have gone out of her way to make her feel welcome. Instead, every time she spoke to her, Hannah replied curtly. After a while, Arleta gave up making the effort.

The other reason she was eager to get back to the house was because she'd had such a good conversation with Noah earlier that morning, and she figured once it started to rain, he'd have to return home early, too. She was hoping after their Saturday chores were done, he'd want to visit with her and his grandmother. Maybe the trio would play a game, although just having an unhurried conversation together would have been a treat.

"I wonder what's keeping Noah," she remarked, glancing out the window as she thought about him now.

"He probably waited out the storm in his buggy and now that the rain's let up, he's back to work again." Sovilla leaned forward in her chair and wagged a finger at Arleta. "But don't change the subject. You were telling me about Isaiah giving you a ride home…"

Arleta understood what kind of information she was fishing for, so she pointedly stated, "There isn't really anything more to say about that. Isaiah is a nice *mann*— he reminds me of my *brieder.*" She must have gotten her point across that she wasn't interested in him romantically because Sovilla relaxed against the cushion and took another sip of tea, a self-satisfied smile on her lips.

"When does the restaurant open?"

"It opens to the public in two weeks from *Muundaag.* But the Millers are hosting a potluck for the entire *kurrich* two weeks from today as a celebration." She told Sovilla that the family intended to have a time of prayer, asking the Lord to bless their business and their customers, followed by supper. Then they'd sing and roast marshmallows in the large outdoor firepit by the pond on the land behind the building.

"*Wunderbaar.* What do you want to make to bring?" Sovilla asked.

Arleta understood why Noah's grandmother wanted to attend—having just been released from near isolation, she undoubtedly was eager to socialize with her community in a festive environment again. But Hannah's chilliness toward Arleta made her wish *she* didn't have to accompany Sovilla to the event. *It will be different with the entire* kurrich *there—even if Hannah doesn't want to talk to me, there will be plenty of other people who will,* she reminded herself. *Besides, Sovilla will be there.*

She wondered if there was any chance Noah would show up at the potluck when he was done with his side projects for the day. Again, she felt a twinge of conscience, because she kind of hoped he wouldn't, since she had lost all her enthusiasm for helping him rekindle his romance with Hannah.

I just don't think she'd be a gut *match for him,* she reflected. Actually, Arleta couldn't really picture him with Honor, either. Nor with any of the women she'd met at church. *But there's always the possibility someone will have a single female relative his age visiting New Hope, and if that were to happen, Sovilla would jump at the opportunity to push them together,* she speculated.

The idea filled her with melancholy, which in turn filled her with shame. Sovilla dearly wanted her grandson to live a full life, a life that included the joy of having a family of his own. And Arleta cared about Sovilla and Noah, and wanted God's best for both of them. So then, why did she suddenly have such a stingy attitude about him meeting someone at the potluck? It wasn't as if Arleta was *jealous* that Noah could enter into a courtship and she couldn't, was it?

Where is *he, anyway?* she wondered. It was raining harder now and there was lightning, too. It seemed unlikely that Noah would continue working during such inclement weather. Besides, Arleta had been so upset last night that she'd forgotten to pack him a lunch, the way she usually did. If for no other reason, it seemed he would have hurried home to eat.

I know what I'll do—I'll make beef casserole for supper, since that's his favorite and he'll be famished.

Even though Sovilla insisted smells no longer bothered her the way they used to, Arleta opened the front door to let the fresh air in as she chopped the onions. She intended to have all of the ingredients ready so she could put the casserole together the minute he got home; because of his work schedule, he'd eaten so many reheated leftovers that for once she wanted him to have a meal straight from the oven. Once she'd prepped everything for the casserole, she decided to make a batch of oatmeal raisin cookies, too, since Noah had once mentioned how much he liked those.

"We're not sticking to a strictly healthy meal plan tonight," she apologetically told Sovilla.

"Am I ever *hallich* to hear that," Sovilla uttered. "I've almost forgotten what dessert tastes like."

Arleta giggled. "It hasn't been *that* long since I've made a treat, has it?"

"*Neh*, I suppose not. But you reminded me to tell you when I got a craving for bumbleberry pie…and I think the time has *kumme*."

"*Jah*, I'll make you one as soon as the berries are in season. For now, these cookies will have to tide you over."

"Just don't let Noah see where you keep them or they'll be gone faster than you can say *schnickelfritz*."

"It's okay. I'll hide the cookie jar in the bottom cupboard. He'll never look there—he's too tall."

But Sovilla needn't have worried; Noah still hadn't arrived after the cookies had cooled and been put away and he didn't show up for supper, either. In fact, he didn't come through the door until his usual time, eight o'clock.

"We were beginning to worry that you'd floated downstream," Sovilla joked, referring to the day's deluge.

"You must be *hungerich*. I've kept your meal warming in the oven. I'll fix a plate for you," Arleta said, eager to surprise him with his favorite foods.

"*Denki*, but I already ate. I'm stuffed." He hung his wet hat on a peg by the door.

"The *Englischers* at Grandview Estates invited you to supper?" Sovilla sounded incredulous, as if the notion of Noah dining with *Englischers* was absurd. Which struck Arleta as strange, considering he ate side by side with Mike Hall every day. He accepted rides in his truck a couple times a week, too. Sometimes it seemed to her that Amish people had double standards regarding their associations with *Englischers*.

"*Neh*. I ate at the Millers' *haus*. Hannah made beef casserole."

"What a coincidence—that's what Arleta made, too," Sovilla said with a chuckle.

But Arleta didn't find it funny; she found it disappointing. Not just that her surprise was ruined, but that Noah had gone to Hannah's house in the first place. She didn't want to appear overly nosy, so she couldn't ask him outright why he'd visited her. Fortunately, however, Sovilla had no compunction about questioning him. "How did you wind up at the Millers'? They don't live anywhere near Grandview Estates."

"I—I—I—" Noah stuttered and his ears turned deep

crimson; if he was trying to hide how embarrassed he was, his body language was giving him away. "I had to quit working on the playhouse because of the storm, so I went to the restaurant to pitch in. There was a leak in the roof so I helped the Miller *buwe* repair it. But we kept having to stop and *kumme* back inside because of the lightning and rain. Eventually everyone except for Jonathan Miller and me went home. Since his *brieder* and Hannah left him without a buggy, once we were finished I gave him a ride back to their *haus* and their *mamm* insisted I stay for supper."

Arleta immediately suspected it was Hannah, not her mother, who really wanted Noah to stay for supper. Without thinking, she blurted out, "Hannah told us her *mamm* has been bedridden for the past week. Is she better now?"

What she was challenging was how Hannah's mother could have insisted he stay for supper if she couldn't even get out of bed. But Noah apparently thought Arleta was suggesting he shouldn't have been around her if she was ill, because she might be contagious.

"*Neh*, she's not completely better yet. But I don't think I could have picked up any germs. I wasn't anywhere near her and she only stuck her head into the kitchen for a minute."

Did Hannah's mamm *also suggest her* dochder *serve beef casserole for supper?* Arleta wryly questioned him in her mind.

She found that hard to believe. It was far more probable that Hannah had recalled how much Noah liked beef casserole from when they were courting, so she'd made it especially for him. Arleta should know; she'd done the same thing herself.

But I did it because I appreciate how hard Noah works and how hungerich *he'd be when he got home. I think Hannah did it because she* likes *him and she wants him for a suitor again,* she deduced. *That has to be the reason she acts so aloof around me—she's annoyed that I'm living here.*

Arleta was sure of it now. And given how ill at ease Noah seemed, she was fairly confident he was keeping something from her and his grandmother. *It must be that he's developing feelings for Hannah again,* she surmised. *What else could cause him to fidget like that?*

Noah momentarily felt as if Arleta could see right through him. But that was ridiculous; there was no way she could have known he'd gone to the frolic specifically to interfere with what he suspected was a blossoming romance between her and Isaiah. So maybe that little frown dragging down her countenance was because she thought it was hypocritical of him to be around Hannah's mother when he'd emphatically told her that she and Sovilla should avoid people who were ill.

Or maybe her expression was a reflection of his own discomfort. For all he knew, she felt embarrassed because she realized that their peers would have told him she'd gotten a ride home with Isaiah. Regardless, there was no way of knowing for sure what was on her mind. He was tired and his stomach hurt—it must have been from eating Honor's *kuchen.* So he excused himself to take a shower and then go upstairs for the night.

Once he was in bed, he reflected on the events of the day. Of all the challenging situations he'd encountered—his conversation with Arleta that morning, the installation setback because of the rainstorm, the leak in the restaurant roof—none was as difficult as eating supper with the Millers.

I never should have stayed, he thought. But when he'd gone inside to see if one of the boys had accidentally exchanged his straight edge for theirs, Eliza Miller had heard him talking and she'd gotten out of bed to personally invite him to supper. She'd been one of his mother's closest friends in New Hope, and she was so grateful for the work he'd done to repair the roof on the restaurant that Noah felt it would have been rude not to accept her invitation.

Surprisingly, eating a meal with the Millers hadn't been painful because being with Hannah reminded him of the night of the fire. It had been painful because being with the boys and their father reminded Noah of being with *his* brothers and dad. He'd gone so long without that kind of rambunctious camaraderie at the supper table that he hadn't realized how much he'd missed it until he had it again, and then his lonesomeness had felt overwhelming.

Noah had always loved being one of four children in his family, and he'd always hoped to have at least that many children of his own... But he knew there was no sense dwelling on what was gone from the past or impossible in the future. He had to refocus on his present goal—earning enough money to take care of his grandmother's medical expenses. *The problem is that*

I got distracted by all this thinking and talking about socializing. I can't believe that I even tried to prevent Isaiah from becoming Arleta's suitor, he marveled. So before rolling over and going to sleep, he resolved that from now on he was going to concentrate solely on his customers again, no matter what anyone else—Jacob, his grandmother, Arleta or even Isaiah—said or did.

The following morning the air was muggy and the sun was blazing—an oppressive combination. Seeing Arleta lace up her boots before they set out for church, Noah remarked, "Didn't you bring any sandals? They'd be a lot cooler." In many places, Amish women—especially the older generation—wouldn't dream of coming to church in sandals, but in New Hope, it was a common practice.

"*Neh.* But these shoes are fine," she replied. She wasn't frowning as she'd been last night, but she wasn't smiling, either.

"Your feet are going to get really hot. Some of the younger *meed* go barefoot. I'm sure no one would think twice if you did, too."

"I'm not a *maedel,* I'm a *weibsmensch.* That's how I prefer to act and that's how I prefer to be treated," Arleta replied hotly as Sovilla held a finger to her lips and shook her head at Noah in the background.

I was just trying to be helpful, he thought, wondering what he'd said wrong. To avoid insulting Arleta again, he didn't speak much on the way to church and neither did she, although Sovilla chatted away enough for all three of them.

The preacher's message was based on a passage from Romans 12, touching on themes of not conforming to the world, not thinking better of yourself than of others, using your gifts in service to the Lord and overcoming evil with good. Noah noticed about halfway through the sermon that his grandmother's eyes were closed, but he didn't wake her. It wasn't uncommon for people to fall asleep during the three-hour service, especially during the warm summer months. The preacher wouldn't be offended if he spotted her dozing, because he knew that worshipping with her district was so important to Sovilla that she'd risked her health to come to church time and again. Noah closed his eyes, too, but not to sleep—he was silently thanking the Lord that Sovilla seemed to be doing so much better now.

After the service ended and lunch had been served and eaten, Noah strolled across the lawn and was hitching the horse and buggy when Arleta approached. "Your *groossmammi* wanted me to tell you she left already. She's going to spend the afternoon at the Stolls' *haus*, catching up with Almeda now that she and Iddo have returned to New Hope again. They'll give her a ride home later this afternoon."

Noah chuckled, realizing Sovilla probably hadn't wanted to tell him herself, because she feared he might have questioned whether it was wise to be out for the entire afternoon. "She's sure making the most of the doctor's *gut* report isn't she? My *groossmammi*'s not letting any moss grow under her feet."

"*Jah*—she seems to be enjoying getting out," Arleta agreed.

While they were talking, Hannah Miller walked up beside her, carrying a round, covered dish in her hands.

She greeted them both, before explaining that she was looking for Sovilla. When Noah told her that his grandmother had already left, Hannah extended the plate to him. "I made this last night—it's bumbleberry pie, in celebration of the improvement in Sovilla's health. She'd mentioned the other day that she hasn't been eating desserts lately, so I thought this might satisfy her sweet tooth. Could you bring it home for her?"

"Sure." Noah was relieved to notice that ever since the hike to the gorge, it was becoming a little easier to make small talk with Hannah. Or at least, the sight of her didn't make him feel quite as guilt-ridden as it used to. Remembering his manners, he added, "*Denki.* It is her favorite, you know."

"*Jah.* I remember that was the reason she gave your *schweschder* and me the recipe—so that if Mary didn't make it for a potluck, there'd always be a chance I would." Hannah added wistfully, "I have such a *gut* memory of that day."

When she blinked and gazed out over the field behind him, Noah was struck with a realization: Hannah had been his sister's closest friend. She'd probably cared about Mary even more than she'd cared about Noah. And he'd been so consumed by guilt and grief that he'd never thought to offer her any consolation after she'd lost her best friend. "Mary was so *hallich* when you moved to town," he acknowledged now, as a sort of belated condolence. "She loved baking with you, and she would have wanted to help with your restaurant."

Hannah met his eyes and nodded and for a moment

Noah thought she was going to cry. But instead she gave him a tiny smile and then said, "See you later."

As she took off across the lawn, Noah addressed Arleta, who was poking at a stick on the grass with the toe of her boot. "You ready to leave?"

"I need to go to the phone shanty to call my *schwe-schder*. I'm going to walk home." She began backing away.

"I'll give you a ride. It's too hot to walk all the way home from the shanty."

"That's okay. Leanna knows I'm going to call, but there's always the chance someone else will be using the phone before us, so I don't want you to have to wait around."

"I'm not in a hurry. I don't mind."

"*I* do—I'd like my privacy," Arleta said sharply. Then she modified her tone. "Besides, you'd better get that pie into a cool place pretty soon or it will spoil."

Noah didn't know what she was so grouchy about today, but he knew a hint when he heard one. So he swiftly got into the buggy, set the pie on the seat beside him and took off for home.

Arleta felt guilty for behaving so miserably—or maybe it was that she was behaving so miserably *because* she felt guilty. Guilty when Noah had drawn attention to her shoes and stockings. Guilty listening to the preacher reading the passage in the Bible about not being conformed to the world. And especially guilty about being so annoyed at Hannah Miller.

Last night she'd lost at least four hours of sleep brooding about why Noah had been asked to stay for supper at the Millers' house yesterday. Arleta had half convinced herself that she'd given the invitation too much significance. She'd reasoned that if Hannah were truly interested in him, she'd be more likely to hide her interest in front of her brothers and parents—not openly invite him to eat supper with them, wouldn't she? Then again, Arleta considered that it was possible Eliza Miller was aware of her daughter's fondness for Noah, so she'd played matchmaker by asking him to dine with them. Back and forth Arleta's thoughts went for half the night and it frustrated her that she couldn't come to any certain conclusion.

Today, however, there was no mistaking Hannah's affection for Noah. *First, she tried to win him over by making beef casserole,* Arleta thought. *Now today she's trying to win his* groossmammi *over with a bumbleberry pie.* A pie she'd made a special effort to bake last night, after having spent the entire day working on the restaurant and then making supper for her family and Noah.

How did she make it anyway? I thought she mentioned she'd used up all of her frozen berries from last season? Arleta grumbled to herself as she cut through a thick stand of pine trees on a shortcut to the shanty. The blackflies were out, and she had to wave her hands around her head to keep them from landing on the exposed skin of her neck—she usually had a severe, although not allergic, reaction to insect bites.

She knew I wanted to make a bumbleberry pie for Sovilla and she knew I haven't been making a lot of sweets lately. So she beat me to the punch. It's as if she was deliberately trying to prove that she's more domes-

tic than I am. And that she'd *make a better wife for Sovilla's grandson or something.* Which was ridiculous, since they weren't in competition; Arleta certainly had no desire to be courted by Noah or to become his wife.

But if that was true, then why had she felt so upset when she noticed the look he gave Hannah as they were reminiscing about the day Sovilla taught her how to make bumbleberry pie? It was obvious the two of them had shared a strong connection while they were courting. And from the tone of their discussion in the churchyard, it was just as obvious they still had deep feelings for each other.

But I am not *envious of her,* Arleta told herself. *I'm hurt that she's been so cold to me, while being so syrupy toward Noah and Sovilla.*

She lifted a low branch so she could pass beneath it, careful not to disturb a spiderweb. When she stood up straight on the other side, she realized she'd happened upon a little brook. She had been so preoccupied with her ruminations that she hadn't heard the current tinkling over the stones, but as she drew nearer, its music danced in her ears.

Stopping on the embankment, she gazed at the sparkling stream of water. It wasn't more than six or eight inches deep and a couple of feet wide. She easily could have crossed it without getting her feet wet—a flat, dry rock protruded right in the middle and she could have stepped on that. But she didn't think she was headed in the right direction because she didn't recall a stream the last time she'd taken this route. *I'll have to turn around,* she thought. *But first, I'm going to cool off.*

She unlaced her boots and then rolled her socks off

and tucked them inside. Her feet were pale and tender, and she inched down the rocky slope toward the water. At first, she just dipped her toes in and the coldness made her nerves tingle straight. Then she boldly plunged both feet into the water. "This is *wunderbaar!*" she shouted.

Holding the skirt of her dress up so she wouldn't get the hem wet, she wiggled her toes. Then she kicked upward, laughing when she sprayed herself with icy droplets. Had she ever felt as refreshed before in her life as she did now? *I regret everything about getting my tattoo except for this one moment*, she thought, aware that if she hadn't worn socks on her feet for almost two years straight, she never would have appreciated just quite how freeing it was to take them off and dunk her feet in a glacial stream.

She took a few steps forward, but the bottom of the stream was comprised of small, sharp-edged rocks and her soles were too delicate to walk on them, so instead she perched on the flat rock in the middle of the stream. Dangling her feet into the water, she closed her eyes and inhaled the pine scent of the air. Five, ten, fifteen minutes passed and with each one, Arleta became more and more aware of how ungodly her thoughts toward Hannah had been.

Reflecting on the preacher's sermon from this morning, she recalled what he'd read in the book of Romans about living at peace with others and being "kindly affectioned" to them. *Oh, Lord, I'm sorry for my attitude toward Hannah*, she prayed. *I am envious of her. I'm envious of Noah, too, because they can court and fall in love and get married and I can't.*

She burst into tears and lay back on the rock's surface, covering her face with her arms for several minutes. Eventually, she dried her eyes on her sleeve and placed her hands at her sides. Looking up through the trees at the sky, she said, "*Gott*, please help me desire and rejoice in what's best for Hannah and Noah. Please help me to be a better friend to both of them." She swished her feet through the water a couple of times before adding, "And *denki*, Lord, for refreshing my body and renewing my mind."

Noah couldn't remember the last time he'd spent a Sunday afternoon alone at home, and he didn't know quite what to do with himself. *This is what it's going to be like after* Groossmammi *dies and I'm all alone.* The thought came out of nowhere, and it made him shiver even though his shirt was sticky with sweat.

He tried taking a nap, but the upper level of the house was so hot he couldn't sleep. So he came downstairs and reclined on the sofa, rereading the passage in Romans that the preacher had read that morning before finally setting the Bible on the end table and nodding off.

It seemed as if no time had passed when he woke with a start and glanced at the battery-operated clock on the mantel-piece: 5:15. The house was completely quiet—hadn't Arleta or Sovilla returned yet? "Anyone home?" he called, but his question went unanswered. Maybe they'd come back and were napping, too?

But when he walked down the hall to the bathroom, he noticed their doors were open and their rooms were empty. Groggy and uncomfortably warm, he splashed water on his face and then went out to the barn for the second milking. *I'm sure* Groossmammi *is fine—she's with Iddo and Almeda and they'll both take* gut *care of her*, he reasoned. *But I wonder what's keeping Arleta? She should have been back a long time ago.*

It occurred to him that maybe she'd come home and left again, so when he went back into the house, he checked the kitchen counters and living room end tables for a note, but there was no indication she'd returned. *I hope she's okay*, he thought as he tromped outside and began pacing on the porch. He considered going out in the buggy to search for her. But even if he left a note telling his grandmother where he went, Noah didn't want Sovilla to return to an empty house. She'd gone all day without a nap—excluding the brief snooze she'd taken in church—and she might be tired and weak and need assistance getting around.

After uttering a prayer for Arleta's safety, Noah decided to go heat up the leftovers so their supper would be ready when they returned. He opened the door to the gas-powered refrigerator, withdrew a large covered dish and peeked inside. Arleta's beef casserole. Even though he'd had it the night before at the Millers' house, his mouth watered; Hannah's casserole was good, but it didn't compare to Arleta's. He just hoped there'd still be enough leftovers so he could take some with him to work tomorrow and eat them cold for lunch.

While the casserole was heating, he pulled out the plates and utensils and set them on the table. Fixing supper temporarily distracted him from worrying about whether something had happened to Arleta. But after he'd placed the water glasses and pitcher on the table and she still hadn't returned, he decided he'd better turn off the oven after all and go look for her.

Right after he twisted the dial, Noah heard a buggy pull up the driveway. He dashed out onto the porch to see Iddo helping Sovilla down from the carriage. Noah hopped down the steps to exchange pleasantries with the deacon and his wife. After the couple's buggy pulled down the lane, he took his grandmother's arm and supported her up the porch stairs.

"I have to sit here to rest a minute before I go any farther," she told him, settling onto the bench. "Could you ask Arleta to bring me a glass of water?"

"She's not home—I'll get it."

Before he reached the door, Sovilla questioned, "Where did she go?"

"I'm not sure. The last I spoke to her she was—"

He was interrupted by the sound of a buggy rounding the bend. It turned up the driveway, pulled by the same horse that Noah had seen hitched at the restaurant yesterday—Isaiah's. *I don't believe this*, he thought. *For the past hour I've been worried about Arleta and she's been out running around with Isaiah?*

He was so irritated he hardly looked at her as she got out of the carriage. Unfortunately, his grandmother waved to Isaiah, calling, "Is that you, Isaiah Wittmer? *Kumme* say hello."

If Arleta had any intention of keeping her courtship with Isaiah a secret, the cat is definitely out of the bag now, Noah thought. But as she bounded up the steps, she didn't seem ruffled in the least; she was practically *glowing*.

"Hi, Sovilla. Hi, Noah," she greeted them. "I hope you weren't too worried about me."

"I just got home—why would I have been worried?" Sovilla said.

By then Isaiah had secured his horse to the fence, and he clomped up the steps and greeted them, too, a complacent grin lighting his eyes.

"Did something happen, Arleta?" Sovilla asked again.

"I got lost in the woods on the way to the phone shanty to call my *schweschder*," she explained. "I came out on the wrong side, over by the Wittmers' farm."

"She was confused because while she was in the woods, she stumbled across a stream and she didn't recall there being one the last time she took that short-cut," Isaiah added.

"*Jah.* Isaiah told me it's too small to have a name and that its bed is dry most of the year, which is why I didn't remember it. It's only running now because of the heavy rains we've had. When I reached it, I tried to backtrack but I got all turned around. Eventually I ended up on the western edge of the Wittmers' property," Arleta said. "Anyway, I'd been wandering around for a couple of hours, so Isaiah gave me a ride home."

"That was kind, Isaiah," Sovilla said. "As long as you're here, you ought to *kumme* in for supper."

Isaiah sniffed the air. "I think I will—it smells *appenditlich*."

Sovilla and Arleta exchanged quizzical looks, so Noah told them he was heating the leftover casserole.

"Great," Arleta said. "I made oatmeal raisin cookies yesterday, too. We can have them for dessert—unless you want to share your bumbleberry pie, Sovilla."

"What bumbleberry pie?" she asked as she led everyone inside. When Arleta told her Hannah had prepared it for her, she said, "I'd be *hallich* to share. But Isaiah is our guest. He can decide what dessert we should have."

"Well, considering I had *kuchen* yesterday at the frolic, I think I'd like cookies tonight, please."

Arleta was all smiles. "Sounds *gut*, but you and Noah will have to close your eyes while I take the cookie jar out of its hiding place," she said, causing Isaiah to laugh heartily.

For a brief moment, Noah had a peculiar misgiving about Arleta's account of getting lost in the woods. This afternoon she had been so insistent that she walk home on such a hot day that it caused him to wonder, *Did she really get lost or had she planned all along to pop in on Isaiah?* The niggling doubt reminded him of how he'd felt after Isaiah had offered to carry Arleta across the stream; something felt amiss but he couldn't put a finger on it.

But then he dismissed his qualm, reminding himself all that was important was that she was home safe. Even if she *had* connived a way to get together with Isaiah, it was none of Noah's business. *My business is earning money so* Groossmammi *can get medical treatments in Mexico if she needs to*, he declared inwardly. *And the sooner we eat supper, the sooner I can go to bed and start a new day of work.*

Chapter Seven

Arleta felt so relieved after she'd confessed her envy of Hannah to the Lord that she decided she was going to do everything she could to encourage Noah to attend the potluck at the Millers' restaurant in two weeks. She didn't have as many opportunities to talk to him about it as she would have liked because he began working even longer hours, and he often showered and went straight to bed when he came home in the evenings. But she dropped as many hints about it as she could without nagging him, and Sovilla added her two cents, too.

Meanwhile, the days flew by. The strawberries and raspberries were ripe, and she spent several mornings picking at a local farm owned by a co-op of Amish families. In the afternoons, Sovilla would wash and slice the berries and then Arleta took over the jam-making and canning processes, since the older woman still didn't quite have enough stamina to be on her feet for that long.

When Arleta called to talk to her mother and sister one afternoon on the way home from purchasing more jar lids, she learned that they'd been making jam and preserving fruit, too. "I miss having your help around here," Leanna complained. "Especially since *Mamm* has been sick."

"*Mamm* is sick?" Arleta repeated, alarmed. "What's wrong with her?"

"It's only a forty-eight-hour bug. I had it last week, too. Everyone around here has been getting it, but it passes quickly. Especially for the *buwe*—I think their stomachs are made of steel."

Arleta chuckled, happy that her mother wasn't seriously ill. "Well, it's *gut* that you're finished with *schul* now, so you're home during the day to help *Mamm*."

"*Jah*, but I may not be home for the entire summer. You'll never guess what I'm going to do."

Arleta figured her sister must have been planning to visit their relatives in upstate New York. "Are you going to *Ant* Betty and *Onkel* Eli's *haus*?"

"*Neh*, nothing quite as exciting as that," her sister answered with a wistful sigh. "I'm going to babysit for an *Englisch familye* who comes to Serenity Ridge for the summer. They have twin *buwe* and one *dochder*."

Her sister's news roiled Arleta's stomach, and she pressed her hand against her abdomen. "Y-you are?"

"*Jah*, if *Mamm* and *Daed* agree to it. But I don't think they'll say *neh*, since it's only for a couple of weeks and the Greens will provide me transportation both ways."

"But why would you do that? Are *Mamm* and *Daed* having money problems? Because I've been saving and—"

"*Neh*, it's not that. It's because Emma's *mamm* has something called a pituitary tumor and she's having surgery. Emma's *schweschder* is going to take a few weeks off her job at the restaurant to care for her and their little *brieder*, first. Then Emma will take a turn staying home in the middle of August. That's when I'm going to fill in for her."

Arleta knew Emma's father had died two years ago and her family had been struggling to make ends meet, even with abundant help from their community. So it made sense that Emma would need to work now that she was finished with school. Because Serenity Ridge, like the other Amish communities in Maine, was a relatively new and small district, jobs for young women were scarce. Arleta understood why Emma needed to work out of their community, for an *Englisch* employer. However, she couldn't comprehend why it was necessary for Leanna to fill in for her.

"Can't the *Englisch familye* hire an *Englischer* while Emma's gone?" she asked.

"*Neh.* They told Emma that they have a very high regard for the way we Amish people raise our *kinner*, so they really don't want anyone else to babysit for them."

"I'm sure if they put their minds to it, they can find a suitable *Englisch* nanny for a couple of weeks," Arleta argued. "I don't think it's wise for you to work for them."

"Why not? *You* worked for an *Englisch familye*, and you loved it."

Exactly, Arleta thought. Somehow, she was going to have to convince her sister—and possibly her parents— that allowing Leanna to work out wasn't a good idea, even if it was beneficial to Emma's family. She gently discouraged her, saying, "I love working for an Amish *familye* so much more. I didn't know it at the time because I had no outside work experience to compare it to. But if I had to do it all over again, I'd never work for an *Englisch* family."

"I'm not too *hallich* about the idea, either," Leanna admitted. "I didn't want to tell you this, but, well, the only reason I'm doing it is so I can give the money to Emma. I know she's really worried about her *mamm*, and their *familye* has already gone through so much. Besides praying, this is the only thing I can do that will really help her."

Arleta squeezed her eyes shut and two hot tears rolled down her cheeks as she contemplated her dear, sweet sister's generosity toward her friend. She sniffed and dropped the subject for now, instead telling Leanna about the upcoming potluck at the Millers' restaurant.

"Will the potato *bauer* be there?" her sister asked.

"*Jah*, probably. But don't worry. As I said, I'm not interested in him and nothing or no one will keep me from returning home at the end of the summer. I promise."

"Oh." There was silence on the other end of the line.

"What's wrong?"

"It's just that you were right… I *have* kind of gotten used to having the entire bedroom to myself."

"Hey!" Arleta exclaimed.

Her sister giggled and quickly reassured her she was just kidding. "I miss you a lot."

"I miss you, too." Arleta knew it was time to get back to Sovilla now, but she could tell there was something else on Leanna's mind. "Are you sure *Mamm*'s getting better?"

"*Jah*, I'm sure."

"Then what's wrong?"

"I…I'm worried about your feet being cold all the

time. Emma's *mamm* couldn't stand being cold, either, and they thought it was because of her thyroid but now she has this pituitary tumor," Leanna blurted out. It sounded as if she was on the brink of crying.

Arleta was, too. She choked back a sob and her eyes filled. She assured her sister that she was perfectly healthy but then, after they'd hung up, she allowed her tears to flow freely. As guilty as she'd felt about getting a tattoo, it didn't compare to the guilt she felt about Leanna worrying that Arleta might have been seriously ill. *I haven't been seriously ill—I've been seriously sinful,* she silently cried. *My deception about my tattoo is even worse than the tattoo itself. And my innocent, trusting* schweschder *has absolutely no idea.*

Arleta was tempted to tell her the truth in order to put her mind completely at ease. But if Arleta disclosed the real reason why she always wore socks, it might give Leanna ideas about going astray, too—especially once she faced the kinds of situations that she was bound to encounter while working with *Englischers.*

What am I going to do? she wondered, climbing back into the buggy. As she headed home, she came up with a plan: if she couldn't dissuade her sister from baby-sitting for the *Englischers,* she'd find out how much money Leanna would earn and *she'd* give that amount to Leanna to give to Emma's family. Which might mean Arleta wouldn't be able to save enough by the end of the summer to have her tattoo removed, but it would be worth it if it spared her sister from being tempted in some of the same ways Arleta had been tempted. She could always earn a little more money here and there with sewing projects or selling baked goods. *As for the* Englischers, *they'll just have to settle for a different babysitter for two weeks*, she thought. *Better that they should compromise their standards than my* schweschder *should compromise her beliefs.*

It was Friday afternoon and Noah was bone tired. He had been putting in extra-long hours for the past two weeks. *It's paying off, though*, he thought as he mentally calculated how much money he'd saved so far compared to the amount he still needed to cover the estimated expenses of a trip to Mexico. He was exactly on target for where he needed to be financially at this point. *If I can pick up the pace tomorrow, I'll be able to complete the pool* haus *roof on Walnut Street and move on to installing the shed roof on South Main...*

A boom of thunder broke through his thoughts and he felt the building—a public gym that was scheduled to open in two months—vibrate beneath him. He and his crewmates gathered their supplies and clambered down just in time to take shelter inside, since the owner had given Noah the key so they could store their tools and materials there while they were working on the installation.

"Look at that dark cloud. We might as well go home now," Jacob suggested, standing in front of the ceiling-to-floor windows. "It's already three o'clock."

"*Neh*, I think it's going to pass," Noah objected. "Let's wait a few minutes."

"I'm *hungerich*," the teenager complained. "Does anyone have anything to eat?"

"Yeah, I've got a steak in one pocket and an ice cream cone in the other," Mike said, razzing him.

Since Noah had worked through their lunch break without eating, his stomach was starting to growl, too. However, because the worksite was so far from their homes, Mike had given his Amish coworkers a ride and Noah's cooler was still in his truck. "I've got a big slice of strawberry pie in my cooler. You can have it once the rain stops," he offered Jacob.

"Why wait?" The young man was out the door and back in a flash, but he still got drenched. He removed his hat and shook his head and upper body like a wet dog before opening the cooler. "Look at all this food Arleta packs for him," he said in amazement to David and Mike. "This is three times as much as my *ants* send with me."

"That's because I'm usually not home for supper." Noah reached in to pull out a container of fried chicken and potato salad. Since there was only one fork, he used it for the potato salad and Jacob ate the pie with his hands, which was what the Amish in New Hope often did during after-church lunches, too. "I think she packed a couple of roast beef sandwiches if either of you want one, David and Mike."

They rummaged through the cooler, selected what they wanted and then the four men sat down in a row, leaning against the wall. While they ate, David told them about the horse he was training and Mike described going deep-sea fishing for the first time the previous weekend. As Noah stuck a fork into a potato and lifted it to his lips—Isaiah was right; Arleta made especially delectable potato salad—it occurred to him that he hadn't had time to go fishing or canoeing at all this spring or summer. He hadn't thought twice about it until he'd heard his coworkers talking about their hobbies and interests. *Maybe later in the summer I'll get the chance to go*, he thought. Listening to the other men, Noah rested his head against the wall and his shoulders relaxed as he enjoyed the conversation and company of his crew.

They polished off their food in no time and then passed around the cooler again, until it was completely empty.

"Tell Arleta that pie was *appenditlich*," Jacob said. "Is she making it for the potluck tomorrow night?"

"I'm not sure," Noah replied.

Every time he'd come home, no matter how late it was, Arleta and Sovilla seemed to be having the same discussion about what main dish Arleta should bring to the potluck and what she ought to make for a dessert. At first, Noah was baffled by their ongoing indecision, but then he realized they were probably just talking about the menu as an excuse to bring up the subject of the potluck. He figured Arleta was excited about the event because she'd get to see Isaiah in a social setting again. And that Sovilla kept mentioning it because she didn't want Noah to forget when it was, in case he changed his mind about going. After a while, he tuned them out, so he never did hear what dish and dessert they'd finally decided to bring.

"I guess we'll find out when we get there." Jacob belched and patted his stomach. "You're going to go, aren't you?"

"*Neh*. I've got to work late tomorrow."

"That's okay—the best *schpass* will start after dark

anyway. Some of us are staying to clean up and then we're going to set off fireworks over the pond behind the restaurant. You should *kumme* for that."

If by "some of us" Jacob meant the same group of single people who had gone hiking at the gorge several weeks ago, Noah wasn't interested. Even though he felt slightly more comfortable around Hannah now, he didn't want to get distracted by the flirtations going on between various members of that group again. "I'm usually beat by the time I'm done working on Saturday."

"That's exactly why you should *kumme* to the potluck." Surprisingly, it was David, not Jacob, who urged him to reconsider. "You're working yourself too hard."

"He's working *us* too hard, too," Mike griped, but it was clear from his smile that he was kidding.

"Yeah, you can say that again," Jacob chimed in. He pointed out the window. "See that? The rain's coming down in sheets. You should let us go home for the day. We'll *kumme* in early on *Muundaag*."

Somehow, Noah doubted that but Jacob was right about the weather; if anything, it was raining even harder now. "All right," he agreed. "Let's go."

So Mike drove them home, pulling up in front of Noah's house last. "Hey, I know I probably shouldn't say this, but David and Jacob are right—you look like you could use a break."

Noah appreciated his coworker's well-intentioned sentiment. "Don't worry. I'm going to take a break on the Sabbath—the day of rest."

"Getting enough rest is an important part of taking a break, but it's just as important to kick back and have some fun once in a while—especially since fireworks and food are involved," Mike said. "If I were Amish, I'd be the first one in line at that potluck supper."

"If you were Amish, there wouldn't be anything left for the rest of us to eat," Noah replied, laughing as he got out of the truck.

He went into the house where Sovilla was filling a glass at the kitchen sink. She turned toward him and lifted a finger to her lips. "Sarah's here with the *bobbel*. He's finally fallen asleep."

Noah nodded, slid off his boots and tiptoed into the living room behind his grandmother. He softly greeted Sarah, who was sitting on the sofa, before he noticed Arleta standing on the opposite side of the braided rug. She cradled the baby in her arms, swaying back and forth ever so slightly. Although the weather outside was dreary, her smile seemed to illuminate the dim room when she looked at Noah and mouthed the words, Kumme *see him*.

He crept forward and peered over her shoulder as she tilted the baby so he could see his face. But when he gazed down, what captured his attention was *Arleta's* expression as she beheld the baby. In that instant she looked so…so *maternal* that he felt both smitten and repelled. Smitten because he could imagine her as a mother and a wife. And repelled because he couldn't imagine *himself* as a father and a husband.

When she blinked her fair, wispy lashes and then angled her face so her eyes met his, he felt as if his knees were about to buckle. "Isn't he *schnuck*?" she whispered.

Noah's mouth was parched. *"Jah,"* he croaked.

"Do you want to hold him? He's fast asleep now."

"*Neh.* I'd better not. I haven't washed up and I need to…to take care of the livestock." Fortunately, his legs held out long enough for him to put his boots back on and shuffle outside, across the yard to the barn. There he plopped down on a hay bale. Resting his forearms against his thighs, he leaned forward, absently staring down at the dirt floor. Droplets darkened the ground between his legs, and he felt so despondent that they could have been his tears. But it was only rainwater, dripping from the ends of his hair because he'd left the house without donning his hat.

He didn't know how long he perched there, motionless, but when his muscles began to cramp, he rubbed the nape of his neck and prayed, *Please,* Gott, *give me strength to keep going.* He wasn't sure whether he was asking for physical strength to keep going for the day or emotional strength to keep going as a bachelor for the rest of his life. It was probably a little of each.

He slowly shifted into a standing position and began tending to the animals. By the time he returned to the house, Sarah's husband must have picked her and the baby up, because Sovilla and Arleta were alone.

"I'm making pork and asparagus stir-fry," Arleta told him. "I've never made it—I've never even tasted it before—but it's supposed to be a healthy recipe. I hope you like it."

"I—I actually ate my lunch just before I came home." Noah didn't know if that was really why he wasn't hungry, but right now he couldn't imagine swallowing so much as a grain of rice. "I'm going to go shower and then I'm hitting the sack."

"Already? It's only six o'clock," Sovilla protested.

"*Jah*, but you keep telling me I need to get more rest."

Actually, what she'd kept telling him was that he needed to have more *fun*, but instead of pointing that out, she took a different tack, reasoning, "I suppose if you go to bed now, you'll be able to get an earlier start to your day tomorrow. And the sooner you get to work, the sooner you can *kumme* home. You might even be back in time to go to the potluck with us."

Noah could have guaranteed right then that wasn't going to happen, but instead he gave his grandmother and Arleta a weak smile and said good-night.

On Saturday morning, Arleta rose extra early so she could be up before Noah left for work. She figured he'd be especially hungry after going to bed without any supper. And, although it was probably futile, she thought she'd urge him one last time to come to the potluck that evening. She was pinning on her prayer *kapp* when she heard the kitchen door opening—he'd just returned from milking the cow. Knowing he'd probably pour himself a bowl of cereal if she didn't tell him she planned to make scrambled eggs and sausage, she flew down the hall and into the kitchen, where he was standing near the table. Attempting to come to a quick halt, Arleta slid across the floor in her stocking feet and crashed into him. She would have fallen over backward if he hadn't caught her, one hand encircling her waist, the other around her shoulders in an awkward embrace.

"Oops—I'm sorry," she apologized as he stabilized her upright. "Did I hurt you?"

Still holding on to her, his face so close to hers she could distinguish the variegation of blues within the bright irises of his eyes, he answered, "*Neh*. Did you hurt yourself?"

Arleta felt a number of sensations—breathlessness, dizziness, tingling—but none of them was painful. *"Neh."*

He loosened his grip a little. "You steady now?"

"*Jah*, I am."

He dropped his arms and stepped backward. "Where are you off to in such a hurry?"

"Nowhere. I was trying to catch up with you before you left so I could make you a nice hot breakfast. I figured you must be *hungerich* after going to bed without supper."

He looked chagrined. "I, uh, I actually got up around midnight and ate some of that stir-fry."

"Cold?"

He shrugged. "I was afraid if I warmed it on the stove, the smell might wake you and *Groossmammi*."

Arleta appreciated how thoughtful he always was. "Go wash up and I'll put on a pot of *kaffi*. Breakfast will be ready in a few minutes." She half expected him to object, but she was glad when he didn't. She was even gladder he tiptoed down the hall and back again without disturbing Sovilla's slumber. It was a rare treat to get to spend time alone with him. As Arleta prepared breakfast, they chatted about the pool house roof he needed to work on that day and discussed whether Sarah's son looked more like her or her husband. Then Noah told Arleta how much his coworkers enjoyed the feast she'd packed for him the day before.

"That? That was just leftovers," she said modestly. "You must have all been starving—food always tastes better than it really is when you've worked up an appetite."

"*Neh*, it was truly *appenditlich*. Even Jacob said so— and he doesn't usually give compliments or exercise *gut* manners," Noah insisted. "And your roast beef sandwich practically made a convert out of Mike."

"A convert?" Arleta questioned. "Why—is he a vegetarian?"

Noah cracked up. "*Neh*. I meant a convert to the Amish faith—he thinks it would be *wunderbaar* to eat that way all the time. I wouldn't be surprised if he shows up at the potluck wearing a straw hat and suspenders."

Arleta laughed. "Well, if he did he might be sorely disappointed by what I'm bringing."

"You finally decided?"

"Your *groossmammi* decided for me. Four bean salad, peppered deviled eggs and pickled green beans." The dishes were traditional staples at Amish picnics and summer potlucks in New Hope, but they wouldn't necessarily appeal to an *Englischer* like Mike.

"What about dessert?"

"I'm making strawberry-rhubarb coffee cake. I figured a lot of other people would bake pies, so this will be a little different." Arleta recognized this would be the perfect moment to urge Noah to stop by the restaurant after work, but for some reason she felt hesitant to do that. She'd thought that she'd gotten over feeling envious about the possibility that Hannah and Noah might want to rekindle their courtship, and she'd been trying to encourage him to come to the event for the past two weeks. So why was she having a sudden change of heart?

It took all of her willpower to say, "If you intend to come to the restaurant after you get done working, I can make up a plate and put it aside for you. Otherwise, there might not be anything left except for whatever Honor makes."

Noah laughed loudly, but before he could give her a definitive answer, Sovilla padded into the room.

"What's *voll schpass*?" she asked, scratching her head through her scarf. Her hair was beginning to grow back, and she said her scalp itched all the time.

"Private joke." Noah winked at Arleta.

Sovilla's eyes darted back and forth between the two of them. "It must be a really *gut* one," she said, and Arleta quickly turned toward the stove so Sovilla wouldn't notice if her face appeared as red as it felt.

Half an hour later, they'd just finished breakfast when a horn sounded in the driveway. Noah jumped up and went outside. When he returned, he explained that he'd forgotten his toolbox in Mike's truck, so Mike had swung by to drop it off. After swilling down the last of his coffee, Noah said he needed to leave. By then, Sovilla had scurried down the hall to shampoo her itchy scalp, and Arleta was in such a rush to pack Noah's cooler that she never did bring up the subject of the potluck again. Which was a shame, because after Noah left and she stood at the sink washing dishes, she realized how much she really hoped he'd attend—not for Hannah's sake, but for *hers*.

After supper, as she stood near the sink washing dishes again—at the Millers' restaurant this time—

she had that same wish. The potluck had been a time of great fellowship, food and fun, and Arleta had enjoyed getting to know many of the district members better. But she'd kept scanning the dining area, hoping Noah had arrived. And even when the sky began to darken and the adults joined the children outside so they could roast marshmallows at the firepit down by the pond, Arleta continued to keep watch for Noah. *It's not too late*, she thought. *He still might* kumme.

Jacob must have noticed her craning her neck as she dangled a marshmallow on a stick over the flames because he asked, "Are you looking for someone?"

Embarrassed, she didn't answer, instead saying, "I wonder if Sovilla's getting tired. Lovina and Wayne brought us here—they're probably ready to go."

"You're not going to leave, too, are you?" Faith asked. "Some of us are lighting fireworks out over the water after all the *familye* with little *kinner* leave. You should stay."

Arleta was going to say she couldn't because she didn't have a ride home when Jacob echoed, "*Jah*, you should stay. I told Noah about it, too, so he might stop by. If he doesn't, I can drop you off before I take Faith home."

Noah might still be coming! Arleta accepted their invitation and then went back up to the restaurant to make sure Sovilla didn't mind. "If Noah comes, that means you'll be on your own for a few hours. Is that okay?" she asked the older woman.

"Of course it is. I'll be asleep anyway," she replied. "And don't you worry—as soon as I walk *in* the door I'm sending Noah *out* the door. He'll give you a ride home."

Arleta smiled to herself, grateful for Sovilla's persistence in pushing her grandson into a social situation. After walking with her and Lovina to where Wayne was hitching the horse and buggy, Arleta darted back to the pond. Within another hour, the gathering around the firepit had dwindled to Isaiah, Honor, Hannah and her brother Jonathan, Faith, Jacob and Arleta. There was no sign of Noah yet.

As a safety precaution, they were waiting until the fire died out before they brought the fireworks down to the pond anyway, but Isaiah said if Noah didn't arrive in the next fifteen minutes, he was going to have to leave. "I'm beat," he remarked, yawning.

"You sound like an old *mann*," Jacob joked.

"Better an old *mann* than a little *bobbel* like you," Isaiah ribbed him back. Then he pointed at Arleta's feet. Except when she went to church, lately she'd been wearing white cotton socks instead of dark stockings. "Still wearing socks, I see. They're so bright they practically glow in the dark."

Feeling self-conscious that he'd drawn attention to her feet, Arleta joked, "Well, your teeth are so bright that your *smile* practically glows in the dark." Her remark made Isaiah grin even wider.

"I'm *hungerich*," Jacob suddenly announced.

"How could you possibly still be *hungerich*?" Honor questioned him. "I saw you refill your plate five times."

"I'm not *hungerich still*. I'm *hungerich again*. Besides, I ate so much other stuff that I didn't have room in my stomach to try any of the desserts. There has to be a leftover pie or two in the kitchen. Can I go look?" he asked Hannah.

"*I'll* go look. The restaurant opens on *Muundaag* and I don't want you scavenging through the cupboards like a bear," she replied, laughing. "Since everything is spick-and-span in there, I'll bring something out for you to eat it here."

"Meanwhile, you can *kumme* help me get the fireworks, Jacob. I promised my *daed* I'd keep them locked in the storage shed behind the restaurant until all the *kinner* went home," Jonathan told Jacob. "You can give us a hand, too, Isaiah."

"I'll help you get the food, Hannah," Arleta offered.

"Neh," she replied sharply. "I'd like Honor to help me."

Arleta's cheeks stung. She'd hardly spoken to Hannah all evening because they'd both been so busy serving and mingling and cleaning up that they only saw each other in passing. But she'd hoped that if they spent a little one-on-one time together now, Hannah might warm up to her. Arleta hung her head, trying to gather her composure after being slighted yet again.

Once everyone was out of earshot, Faith sidled up to her. "Don't take Hannah's attitude to heart. She's just jealous."

Arleta snapped her head upward, surprised both because Faith had noticed Hannah's curtness and because she had attributed it to jealousy. "Why would she be jealous?"

Just then there was a commotion over in the parking lot—apparently Noah had arrived and the other young men were greeting him. As delighted as Arleta was that he'd finally made it, she urged Faith to answer her question before everyone circled back to the firepit. "Why would she be jealous?" she repeated.

"I shouldn't be telling you this…" Faith whispered. "But you-know-who used to be her suitor and she hoped they'd get married. But he broke it off with her because he didn't feel ready. That was years ago and she was devastated. Then this spring, he started showing signs he was interested in courting her again, but he's the type who needs a lot of…of *encouragement*. He doesn't have as much self-confidence as it seems. But then you showed up and you two get along so well and—"

Faith wasn't able to complete her thought because Noah, Isaiah and Jacob had come within a few yards of them, but Arleta got the picture. It was exactly as she suspected: Hannah had been surly toward her because she thought Arleta was interested in Noah, or vice versa. *It's not my fault that Noah and I get along so well—or that he ended their courtship,* she thought defensively.

Almost immediately, she also remembered that she'd prayed the Lord would help her be a better friend to Noah and Hannah. And even though Arleta didn't think it was fair or kind for Hannah to treat her the way she had, it *was* understandable. She *loved* Noah, after all— she'd hoped to marry him. *I wish there was something I could do to show her that Noah and I aren't interested in each other romantically,* she thought. Yes, she had enjoyed having his arms around her that morning, but that was an accident, not an intentional embrace. Besides, even if she was drawn to him, it wasn't as if Arleta and Noah could ever have a future together. But what could she do to alleviate Hannah's envy?

"Hi, Arleta, hi, Faith," Noah greeted them as he stepped up to the firepit. They said hello back. The flames were almost out so Arleta couldn't see his expression, but she could hear the pleasure in his voice as he said, "I'm *hallich* I got here in time. I haven't lit fireworks for about ten years, and I heard that Hannah's bringing dessert out, too. I'm really looking forward to this."

"*Jah*, but unfortunately, Jonathan forgot the key to the storage shed at his *haus*. He just left to get it," Isaiah explained. "Unfortunately, I'm too tired to stick around until he gets back, so I guess I'll say *gut nacht* now."

"You're not going to stay for dessert—or should I say, for *more* dessert?" Hannah asked. She'd come up behind them, carrying what looked like a box or some type of container.

"*Denki*, but my stomach is already sore from everything else I ate." Isaiah bid everyone goodbye and began hiking up the hill to the parking lot.

Arleta seized the opportunity to show Hannah once and for all that she wasn't interested in Noah. "Do you mind dropping me off, Isaiah?" she called.

"Not at all," he answered, waiting for her to catch up with him.

At the same time, Noah questioned, "You want to leave already? I can give you a ride—"

"*Neh*," she interrupted him. "You just got here and you're looking forward to enjoying the evening with your friends. *Gut nacht*, everyone."

Then she scurried up the hill, as if to prove—contrary to how she actually felt—that she couldn't get away from Noah fast enough.

Chapter Eight

"Arleta and Isaiah seem very fond of each other," Hannah remarked, as if Noah hadn't noticed.

Until now, he had half convinced himself that the time Arleta had gotten a ride home from Isaiah after getting lost in the woods was merely happenstance, but there was nothing coincidental about the way she'd asked Isaiah for a ride home tonight. She'd practically chased him down! Isaiah hadn't seemed to mind her approaching him in front of everyone else like that, but Noah had been taken aback by her boldness. He'd never known an Amish woman to be so blatant about expressing her interest in a man. On occasion—such as in Jacob's case—an Amish man might overtly pursue a young woman romantically, not caring whether his peers witnessed his audacious behavior as he attempted to win her over, but it was never the other way around. If an Amish woman had her eye on someone, she'd be much more subtle about letting him know than Arleta had been.

"*Jah.*" Noah acknowledged Hannah's observation,

but he didn't encourage further discussion. His stomach was sour, and the sight and sound of the fireworks had given him a splitting headache. To make the evening even worse than he could have anticipated, he had been forced to give Hannah a ride after Jonathan confided he wanted to take Honor back to her house without his sister in the buggy. And of course, Jacob and Faith took off together, too. *Everybody is pairing up*, Noah thought. *But what else did I expect?*

Fortunately, the Millers didn't live very far from their restaurant, so it was only a matter of minutes that Noah had to be alone with Hannah in the buggy. After making the remark about Isaiah and Arleta, she clammed up until bidding him good-night when he dropped her off in front of her house. If there was one good thing about having such a bad headache and being so annoyed by Arleta's behavior, it was that it completely distracted Noah from the fact that the last time he'd brought Hannah home was on the night of the fire.

I knew *it was a mistake to hang out with the others after the potluck ended*, Noah thought as he pulled onto the main road. *But I didn't have much of a choice.* When Sovilla had come home and found him eating a late supper of scrambled eggs, she'd insisted he go pick Arleta up. It was just the push he'd needed, as he'd been on the fence about whether or not he ought to try to participate in lighting fireworks, as Jacob had suggested.

Actually, if he were really being honest, Noah would admit that all day he'd been thinking about how he'd caught Arleta in his arms when she'd slipped on the kitchen floor, knocking into him. With the exception of hugging his relatives, that was the first time in his life he'd embraced a woman that closely. Even when he'd kissed Hannah as a teenager, he hadn't put his arms around her—he'd held her hand in his. In a strange way, clutching Arleta so she wouldn't fall felt more meaningful to him than kissing Hannah had felt. Which didn't make any sense. Just as it didn't make any sense for him to believe that Arleta had really wanted his company at the potluck. *She was so intent on running after Isaiah that she hardly even acknowledged me,* he thought.

He'd gone all that way for what? A headache and a raspberry tart he didn't even enjoy because his stomach was doing flips. *That's the last time I'm compromising my better judgment,* he thought. No matter how much his grandmother insisted, cajoled or pleaded, he wasn't going to any more social events with Arleta this summer, not even to pick her up.

In fact, the next morning at the breakfast table when Sovilla asked them if they'd had fun the evening before, he answered bluntly, "*Neh.* I wish I hadn't gone. I wound up with a *baremlich* headache."

"You did? Oh, that's too bad." Arleta clicked her tongue against her teeth. "I thought you were really enjoying yourself and that's why you stayed out late."

"It wasn't that late. But I did have to drop Hannah off at home," Noah started to explain. Then he caught himself, realizing that Jonathan had confided his interest in Honor to him privately, and he wouldn't appreciate it if Noah disclosed his secret to Arleta and Sovilla.

"*Hannah?*" Sovilla cut in, obviously confused. "If

Noah was taking Hannah home, how did you get back here, Arleta?"

"Isaiah gave me a ride."

"I don't understand. Why didn't Noah give you a ride, too?"

Arleta's face turned pink, just like it had on the day when Sovilla announced at breakfast that the young woman didn't have a suitor. Seeing her discomfort, Noah's annoyance at Arleta melted. He realized that while she might not have cared if her peers knew how infatuated she was with Isaiah, she was clearly bashful about talking to Sovilla about it.

"Isaiah was leaving anyway, so Arleta went with him since I wanted to stay longer than she did," he answered for her. "At that point, I didn't have a headache yet."

"Jah," Arleta agreed, giving him a grateful look. "I was tired but I didn't want to spoil Noah's *schpass.*"

Sovilla eyed Arleta and then Noah before shaking her head in apparent disbelief. "I don't understand you two. You're so young and in such *gut* health, yet you act as if you've got anvils tied to your legs, dragging you down. *I'm* supposed to be the one who's old and sickly."

"She sure doesn't *look* sickly, does she?" Arleta asked Noah, eager to change the subject. She knew he wouldn't want to discuss whatever was going on between him and Hannah with Sovilla. And clearly, something *was* going on, since he'd given her a ride home. It was exactly what Arleta hoped would happen, yet now that it had, she didn't particularly want to hear him talk about it, either.

"*Neh*. Her coloring is a lot better now. Her eyes are brighter, too," Noah remarked. "But the real test of how well she's doing and how much energy she has will be whether she can stay awake in *kurrich* this morning."

"Ach! Twenty-three years old and you're still a little *schnickelfritz*!" Sovilla shook her finger at Noah, laughing.

Arleta loved seeing her so energetic. *It must be because she has a ray of hope about her grandson courting again*, she thought. Imagining that Noah's relationship with Hannah had the potential to bring Sovilla joy made Arleta happy, too.

Or at least, it made her *want* to feel happy. But some small part of her felt lonely—felt left out—knowing she couldn't enter into a courtship like the one she'd helped revive between Hannah and Noah. She tried to shake off her low mood but later, as she sat in church listening to the first preacher deliver a sermon based on 1 Timothy about being a good example to others, Arleta grappled with feelings of regret and shame. Then, after worship and lunch were over, she was helping clean up and she tripped, almost dropping the tray of leftover food she was carrying into the kitchen.

Hannah and Faith were standing nearby and they'd seen her stumble so she poked fun at herself, quipping, "Pride goeth before a fall."

"You said it, not me," Faith retorted, causing Hannah to giggle.

Maybe Arleta was being too sensitive, but it sounded as if Faith's jest had an edge to it—as if she truly believed Arleta was a prideful person. And Hannah seemed to be laughing *at* Arleta, not *with* her. *It seems like she should be nicer to me than that, now that it's clear* she's *the one Noah's interested in*, Arleta thought. Her shoulders drooping, she set the tray of food on the counter for someone else to put away and went upstairs to see if Sovilla was ready to leave.

But the older woman informed her that she was going to spend the afternoon visiting with the deacon and his wife at their house. *Sovilla has a more active social life than I do*, Arleta glumly thought. She headed outside and waited in the shade of a maple tree for Noah to pass by on his way to hitch the horse and buggy. As she was standing there, Isaiah approached and her spirits lifted. *At least there's one person my age in New Hope who's always* hallich *to see me.*

Today, however, Isaiah wasn't smiling. "Hello, Arleta," he said in a low voice. "There's, uh, something I'd like to speak with you about in private…"

Fearing he was about to invite her to go for a ride with him—possibly so he could ask to be her suitor—Arleta felt her upper lip and forehead breaking out in beads of sweat. Given her recent behavior, including trailing after him to ask for a ride home last evening, as well as allowing him to carry her across the stream at the gorge, it was understandable that he would have thought she was interested in a courtship with him. But she didn't want him for a suitor. For a friend, yes, but not for a suitor. Trying to stall until she could think of a tactful way to turn him down, she said she'd be happy to chat with him but she wondered if he needed a glass of water, first. "You look a little pale. Do you feel all right?"

"*Neh*, not really. My stomach hurts and I'm not sure if I have the bug that's been going around or if it's from something else. Something that's been weighing heavily on my mind," he admitted.

Oh, neh, she fretted, *I hope he's not going to tell me he's lovesick!* "Well, a lot of people are getting the stomach flu in New Hope. My *schweschder* told me it's going around Serenity Ridge, too. But the *gut* news is that it only lasts two days, tops," she rambled nervously.

When she stopped to take a breath, Isaiah cut in. "*Neh*. I think my stomachache might be because I've been troubled by something I'm ashamed of doing."

That wasn't what Arleta expected him to say, and she wasn't quite sure why he'd want to confess something he was ashamed of to *her*. "Oh?" she uttered.

"*Jah*. You see, I'm afraid I… I'm afraid I may have led you to believe that I might be, uh, might be seeking a courtship with you, but I'm not." He tentatively glanced at her from beneath the brim of his hat.

Arleta at once felt like laughing because she was relieved and like crying because she'd been so vain to imagine Isaiah wanted to be her suitor. *Pride* does *goeth before a fall*, she scolded herself. Tongue-tied once again all she could say was, "Oh?"

"*Jah*. I mean, you're a lot of *schpass* and I enjoy your company, but I kind of think of you as being like a kid *schweschder*. I'm really sorry if I've given you the wrong impression, Arleta." He paused and looked at the ground before meeting her eyes again. "I, uh, I know I can trust you not to say anything about this, but I'm actually interested in courting someone else. I just haven't had the courage to express my feelings to her because... well, because I'm afraid of how she'll respond."

Isaiah appeared utterly miserable and Arleta knew she was to blame for the misunderstanding between them. So instead of telling him she didn't want him for a suitor, anyway, she simply said, "I completely understand and I appreciate your honesty."

"Really? You're not angry at me?"

"*Neh*, I'm not. And I hope we can continue to be friends."

"*Jah*, of course." Isaiah smiled but he still appeared wan, and Arleta regretted that she may have contributed to his distress.

She leaned forward and spoke quietly, as people were beginning to stream past them toward the area where their horses were tied to the long stretch of hitching post. "You know, Isaiah, whatever *weibsmensch* you'd like to court would be fortunate to have you for a suitor. You should take the risk and tell her how you feel."

"I'd like to," he said, "but I'm not as open as you are."

Ha! Arleta laughed contritely to herself. *If he only knew what I'm hiding...*

Noah approached them just then and greeted Isaiah before asking Arleta if she was ready to leave. She was, but after her conversation with Isaiah, she needed time alone to think, so she told Noah she intended to walk, instead. "I might stop at the phone shanty, so don't be surprised if I'm not home for a while."

"I probably won't be there by the time you get back

anyway," he replied before striding away as if he were in a hurry.

He must be taking Hannah out for a ride, Arleta deduced, but of course, she didn't ask him if that's what he planned to do after he went home and changed.

"I hope you don't get lost in the woods again. But if you *kumme* out on the wrong side, feel free to stop in at the farm," Isaiah said with a chuckle, and then he walked away, too.

Within five minutes of leaving the church, Arleta's dress clung to her back and her socks were wet with perspiration, too. She couldn't wait to take them off when she got to the stream in the woods, but the water was even shallower than the first time she'd been there and the mosquitoes were out in full force, so she hurried off to call her family. Since she hadn't arranged to speak with them ahead of time, she reached the voice mail recording for the phone nearest their house in Serenity Ridge but she didn't leave a message. What would she have said? "I'm only calling to let you know a *mann* who wasn't my suitor just broke off a courtship I didn't even have with him"?

"I'm sweltering," she whined plaintively when she walked through the front door to Sovilla and Noah's house thirty minutes later. The first thing she did was remove her shoes and socks, and then she went straight into the bathroom. Sitting on the edge of the tub, she turned on the water and stuck her feet beneath the faucet. She didn't feel quite as refreshed as she'd felt the first time she'd visited the stream, but the water cooled her skin considerably.

I might as well make the most of being in the house alone, she thought, and decided not to put on another pair of socks after drying her feet. She retrieved her stationery, poured herself a glass of lemonade and then wandered outside to sit on the double wooden glider on the porch. The sun was hitting her directly in the eyes, but it was still cooler there than it was in the house so she stayed put.

Too drained to even push the chair back and forth, she sipped her drink and contemplated how she'd phrase a letter to her parents, warning them against allowing Leanna to work out at the *Englischers'* home. But when she drew a blank, she tried to mentally compose a letter to her sister, instead.

She wondered if she should be so candid as to caution her, *If you work with* Englischers*, you might be tempted to start acting like one.* Or, worse, *You might want to* become *one.* No, her sister would scoff at the possibility. Arleta remembered when Jaala, the deacon's wife in Serenity Ridge, had inquired whether she was concerned that her *Englisch* employers might have a bigger influence on Arleta than she had on them. In retrospect, she appreciated that Jaala had cared enough to try to protect her, but at the time, she'd felt insulted.

Maybe she should write, *It's Sunday afternoon and everyone else is out socializing and courting but I'm sitting at home by myself, which is something I expect to do a lot in the future. I have no hope of ever getting married or having children and I feel estranged from my family and community—sometimes I even feel estranged from the Lord. I'm pleading with you not to*

make the same kind of mistakes I made, beginning with
working in an Englischer's *home...*

Arleta wasn't going to tell her sister any of that; she
didn't have the courage. She set her tablet aside and
closed her eyes. Leaning back, she rested her head against
the side of the house, stretched her legs out in front of
her and allowed the tears to flow freely down her face.

The next thing she knew, she felt a shift in temper-
ature as a shadow blocked the sun. "Arleta?" Sovilla
asked, touching her arm.

She sat up with a jerk and swiftly drew her feet back
under the glider, panicked. Had Sovilla seen her ankle?
"I must have dozed off. Have you been standing there
long?"

"*Neh.* I got home about an hour ago. You were sleeping so soundly you didn't hear me go past. I didn't wake
you because you'd said you've been tired, but I shouldn't
have let you sleep so long. It looks as if you've gotten
sunburned. I'll go get an aloe leaf from the fridge."

Arleta touched her cheeks, which were warm. Her
forearms were bright pink and freckling; she'd definitely gotten a burn. But her more pressing concern
was how she was going to get inside and put on a pair
of socks without Sovilla seeing her tattoo.

A minute later, Sovilla returned with a knife and an
aloe leaf, which she cut open so Arleta could spread its
cool gel over her skin. "That feels *wunderbaar*," she
said as she rubbed a generous blob of it onto her fore-
arm. Although the tops of Arleta's feet were hot and
tingling and she knew they were burned, too, she was
relieved that Sovilla didn't suggest that she apply aloe

to them, as well. She kept her legs bent beneath her and her ankles pressed together, out of sight.

"I've got to go take a shower," Sovilla announced, scratching her head. "This heat is making my scalp itchier than usual today."

"I'll be right in as soon as I gather my things," Arleta said. She waited until she heard the bathroom door close before she darted inside to her room and pulled on a pair of socks. The fabric caused the tender skin on her feet to sting, but she figured it was nowhere near the amount of discomfort she would have experienced if Sovilla had discovered her secret.

"Where have you been all afternoon?" Noah's grandmother questioned him when he arrived home just in time to eat supper. Since cooking big meals on the Sabbath wasn't permitted by the *Ordnung*, on Saturday Arleta had set aside some of the four bean salad, peppered deviled eggs and pickled green beans she'd made for the potluck. She'd also baked an extra strawberry-rhubarb coffee cake just for them to enjoy at home.

"I went to Little Loon Pond," he mumbled, his mouth full. After church, he'd returned home to change and pick up his fishing equipment and then he'd journeyed to the pond, which could be accessed from behind his coworker David Hilty's property. The Amish in New Hope kept two communal canoes there for anyone in their district to use. Although he hadn't gotten a single nibble on his line all afternoon, Noah didn't mind. There was a cool, gentle breeze blowing over the water, and as he paddled close to the shaded shoreline, he became more and more relaxed. He hadn't had such a peaceful outing since his grandmother had been diagnosed with cancer. Any residual exasperation he'd felt about Arleta's behavior the previous evening completely dissipated. Afterward, he decided he'd try to go to the pond at least every other Sunday for the rest of the summer, which he hoped would keep Sovilla from badgering him to get out more often.

"Was anyone else there?"

"A few other people, *jah.*" Noah had spotted Honor and Jonathan canoeing, too, but he pretended not to see them in order to give them their privacy. He quickly shifted topics so Sovilla wouldn't question him further. Noticing Arleta was quieter than usual and she was poking at her food instead of eating it, he asked if she was okay.

"I'm a little out of sorts," she mumbled without looking up.

Noah wasn't sure whether she meant she was physically out of sorts or if she was emotionally upset. It occurred to him that she might have had an argument with Isaiah. They'd seemed to be having a very serious conversation when he'd approached them in the churchyard after lunch. Because Arleta had declined a ride home with Noah, he assumed she was either planning to meet up with Isaiah later or hoping he'd offer her a ride once Noah left. Maybe things didn't go according to plan?

That's not for me to wonder about, he reminded himself. However, so many people had been sick from church lately that he did feel justified in asking, "Do you think you've caught the bug that's going around?"

"*Neh.* I think I caught too much sun today." Frowning, she stood up. "I'm sorry, but I have to excuse myself. I'll *kumme* back to clear the table in a little while."

"That's okay, dear. Noah and I can manage. You go lie down. I'll check on you in a little while," Sovilla instructed. The fact that Arleta didn't insist on doing the dishes or object to the older woman's caregiving indicated how ill she must have felt.

"I hope Arleta's all right. I wouldn't want you to catch anything from her," Noah remarked.

"I hope she's all right for her *own* sake, the poor *maedel.*"

Sovilla had a way of scolding Noah for being insensitive without actually saying he was being insensitive. But he couldn't help worrying about his grandmother's health—if Arleta had the flu, she'd get over it in a couple of days. If Sovilla contracted it, she might end up in the hospital.

Groossmammi's come too far in her recovery to suffer a big setback like that now, Noah thought. While protecting his grandmother's health was his top priority and he would spare no expense to keep her well, he didn't want to have to pay for a hospital bill—which would put a big dent in his Mexico trip funds—if hospitalization could be avoided.

"To be on the safe side, I think we should consider asking Arleta to return to Serenity Ridge until she feels better. I seem to remember her telling me her *familye* already had the bug, so they won't catch it. Maybe Lovina would be willing to *kumme* stay with you and cook for a couple of days."

"Don't be *lecherich*! Arleta got too much sun, that's all."

"Maybe, but you can't be too careful, *Groossmammi*. You have a weakened immune system."

His grandmother slowly wiped her lips and set her napkin aside. "Arleta has taken great pains to keep me well. She has kept this *haus* as clean and germ-free as humanly possible, and she's prepared nutritious, *appenditlich* meals. Not to mention, she's put up with all my moods and demands. And now you want to repay her by sending her home when *she's* ill?"

"Her *repayment* is her salary. She earns a lot of money doing all those tasks you just listed!" The words were out of Noah's mouth before he could stop them, and he hardly realized what they sounded like until he noticed his grandmother's disgusted expression.

"I don't care if you're paying her a *million* dollars. Nor do I care whether she's merely sun sick or she has the plague—I am *not* sending her home when she's ill," Sovilla declared. "I trust her to take precautions to keep me from catching any illness she may have, and I trust the Lord to know all of my needs. If you don't, then *you* can ask her to leave. But you'll need to stay home with me until she returns, because I am not imposing on our friends for something I consider an unnecessary measure. So I'd advise you to pray about it and sleep on it before you carry out your plan. Now, if you'll excuse me, I'm going to go reciprocate a tiny bit of the tender care to Arleta that she's shown to me."

After Sovilla tottered down the hall, Noah cleared the table and rinsed the dishes. He didn't know what had gotten into his grandmother. Why did she consider it such an affront to ask Arleta to leave until she was well again? Considering Sovilla's fragile health, it seemed like a reasonable request to make.

Yet a couple of hours later as the suffocating heat in the loft made it difficult for him to breathe, much less to sleep, Noah questioned whether *he* was the one who'd been unreasonable. *I suppose it's possible that Arleta really is suffering from too much sun exposure.* Since he didn't know if she was actually contagious, was sending her away worth upsetting his grandmother and forfeiting three or four days' worth of salary? After praying about it, Noah decided he'd wait until the morning to see if Arleta felt better before he asked her to leave.

He had arranged for Mike to pick everyone up an hour earlier than usual since they'd gone home early on Friday, so the sun hadn't even risen yet when Noah came in from milking the cow. Surprisingly, Arleta was standing at the stove, frying bacon. "*Guder mariye.* You're up early. Does that mean you feel better?" he asked.

"It means I feel *hungerich*," she said, ridding Noah's mind of any worry that she'd had the stomach flu, which typically lasted for two or three days, not for a single evening.

Gut, that's one issue resolved. I just hope by the time I get home I'm not still in hot water with Groossmammi, Noah thought. To help mend the rift between them, right before he went out the door, he wrote Sovilla a note that said, *Dear Grandma, I was wrong and I'm sorry. Signed, Your twenty-three-year-old Schnickel-*

fritz. He folded the paper into a small square and tucked it into her Bible, which she read in the morning daily.

As Mike drove his three coworkers to the site, Jacob informed Noah and David that he'd heard that Isaiah had to go to the ER the previous evening. Apparently he'd caught the stomach bug and had vomited so many times he became severely dehydrated, but he felt a lot better once he received medication and IV fluids.

"That's *baremlich,* but I'm grateful to *Gott* it wasn't something more serious," David replied.

"So am I," Noah emphatically agreed.

Jacob monopolized the conversation the rest of the way to the gym, yammering on about how great the potluck was. "You won't believe it," he said to Mike and David. "But Noah actually showed up—and afterward, he gave a certain *maedel* a ride home."

"You mean Arleta? She's living with his grandmother and him, you know, so that doesn't really count for giving a girl a ride home," Mike said.

"*Neh,* Arleta got a ride from someone else. Noah left with—"

David cut him off midsentence, most likely to spare Noah any embarrassment. "I saw you canoeing on the pond on *Sunndaag,* Noah. Were the fish biting?"

"*Neh.* But I enjoyed paddling around."

"Enough about that. What *I* want to know is if your cooler is filled with potluck leftovers," Mike hinted.

Noah actually had no idea what was in his cooler, since Arleta had packed it while he'd been in the other room writing a note to his grandmother. "You'll just have to wait and see," he replied.

But by the time lunch hour rolled around, Noah didn't feel like eating anything. His head hurt again, and he was so woozy he couldn't stand to watch the other men consume their food—or to work their way through *his* cooler.

After sitting alone in the shade and sipping water for twenty or thirty minutes, his nausea passed and he concluded he'd gotten overheated. *If I didn't know that the sun had affected Arleta the same way, I'd be worried I have the stomach flu,* he thought. He still didn't feel hungry, but since the other men had devoured his lunch, it was just as well.

When he arrived home it was nearly six o'clock and Noah expected to smell supper cooking, but instead he found Arleta sitting on the glider on the porch, wringing her hands. "What's wrong?" he immediately asked.

"I'm afraid your *groossmammi* has been ill. She's sleeping right now, but she's had a very rough afternoon." She described Sovilla's symptoms, which were similar to how *he'd* felt at lunch.

His fists clenched at his sides, Noah tried to remain calm. "Was she outside in the sun a lot today?"

"*Neh.* Except to use the bathroom, she's hardly been out of bed. She's too weak," Arleta explained. "She only has a slight fever, so that's a *gut* sign. I was going to go call the *dokder* to ask if she should make an appointment as a precaution, but I didn't want to leave her on her own. And at first, I thought the vomiting would pass quickly, the way it did for me last night."

Noah couldn't believe his ears. "You got sick to your stomach last night and you didn't tell me?"

Arleta's sunburned cheeks turned an even deeper shade of pink. "I—I—I'm sorry, but I—"

"What *gut* does it do to be sorry? You should have been *safe*!" He paced to the opposite end of the porch and stood staring across the yard, his back toward her. "She'd better not end up in the hospital like Isaiah did!"

Arleta gasped. "Isaiah's in the hospital?"

"*Neh*, not anymore." Noah spun around to face her. "But maybe if you had cared as much about my *groossmammi*'s health as you obviously care about your suitor's, she wouldn't be sick right now. In fact, Isaiah is probably the reason she's sick. You caught the stomach virus from him and passed it on to her!"

"*What* are you talking about?"

"I saw you cozying up to him on *Sunndaag* after *kurrich*, Arleta. And *all* our peers saw you chasing him down on *Samschdaag* evening. If you're that brazen toward him in public, I can only imagine what you're like around him in private—"

"*Absatz!*" Arleta shouted, leaping to her feet. She marched to the door and jerked it open. Before going inside, she paused to say over her shoulder, "Since you don't believe I care about your *groossmammi*'s health, you'll need to find a replacement for me as soon as possible. Meanwhile, I'd appreciate it if you'd keep your opinions about my character to yourself."

Not a problem, Noah thought as she disappeared into the house. *Unless it's absolutely necessary, I don't intend to speak to you at all.*

Chapter Nine

Arleta sobbed into her pillow so Sovilla wouldn't hear her. There was only one time in her life when she'd felt more hurt than she did right now, and that was when Ian broke up with her in a letter. *After all this time, how could Noah suggest I don't care about Sovilla's health?* She considered that to be almost a worse insult than his remark about the way she behaved toward Isaiah, although they were both horrible things for him to say. *I've tried so hard to take care of Sovilla. And I've tried to be a gut Amish role model ever since I was baptized into the kurrich. I haven't done any of it perfectly, but it's just so unfair—so unkind—of Noah to suggest I've done the exact opposite*, she lamented.

And why had he assumed Arleta was the one who'd brought the bug home to his grandmother? Sovilla had received visitors at the house, she'd gone to the potluck and she'd gone to church. It was far more likely that she'd gotten sick from being around someone else in the community than from Arleta, who was hypervigilant about washing her hands and covering her mouth when she coughed or sneezed. She was meticulous about food preparation, too. Most important, Arleta's symptoms were too short-lived to be the flu, she was sure of it.

Sniffling, she rolled over and lay still on her back, listening for movement in the next room. She was relieved to hear faint snoring; that must have meant Sovilla's stomach had settled down enough for her to sleep. Earlier in the evening, Noah had gone to the phone shanty and spoken to the doctor on call at the clinic. She'd told him that as long as Sovilla didn't run a high fever or become dehydrated, there was no need to make an appointment, since the virus would run its course without medication. Still, most people who'd had the flu said the stomach and intestinal issues lasted for a full twenty-four hours, at least, followed by lesser bouts of nausea and weakness. Arleta realized she'd told Noah to find a replacement for her immediately, but she hoped to stay in New Hope until she was sure his grandmother had completely recovered from the flu.

She'd been so upset about what Noah had said and about Sovilla being ill that it hadn't occurred to Arleta until just now that by quitting her job, she had also given up her goal of earning enough money to get her tattoo removed. *It's okay*, she tried to convince herself. *I was going to give Emma's* familye *a portion of my savings anyway, so Leanna won't have to babysit for the* Englischers. Besides, as Noah had indicated, everybody already thought she behaved inappropriately, so what did it matter if she had a tattoo or not? *At this point, I'm done caring about what anyone—especially people who are as unfair as Noah and as cold as Hannah—think about me*, she defiantly decided. *And I'm done wearing socks to bed, too!* She reached down, tugged them off and dropped them on the floor beside her bed. Then, utterly drained, she shut her eyes and went to sleep.

She must have dozed for two or three hours before she was woken by the sound of the bathroom door closing. She bounded out of bed and down the hall to see if Sovilla needed help. But Sovilla's door was shut; that meant it was Noah who was in the bathroom. As Arleta turned to go back to her room, she heard the unmistakable sound of retching: he was ill. *Great. Now he's going to blame me for that, too*, she thought and she slid into bed.

But she lay awake, listening for him to walk past her room on his way back upstairs. After ten or fifteen minutes passed with no sound of him going by, she got up, put on her bathrobe and tiptoed down the hall. Rapping lightly on the bathroom door, she quietly asked, "Are you okay, Noah?" Her question was met with a groan. A few seconds later, the door opened and she realized he wasn't standing in front of her—he was sitting on the floor.

"I feel *baremlich*," he moaned, his eyes bloodshot and his face pale.

She extended her hand. "Here, I'll help you up."

"*Neh.* Not yet."

Understanding what he meant, Arleta replied, "I'll go make up the couch, so you can be closer to the bathroom if you need it."

"*Denki*," he muttered, and abruptly closed the door.

Arleta flew into her room and donned her *kapp* so she could pray for Noah as she brought fresh sheets and a pillow into the living room. No matter how deeply he'd hurt her, it pained Arleta to see him so sick and after turning the couch into a temporary bed, she circled back to the bathroom and knocked on the door again. This time, he took her hand and allowed her to help him into a standing position. He was so unsteady that she had to prop him up all the way into the living room, where he collapsed onto the sofa.

She brought him a glass of cold ginger tea, but he shook his head, apparently too drained to speak. She went back into the kitchen and took ice cubes from the tray. She knew he probably couldn't tolerate more than a few slivers at a time, but she didn't want to wake Sovilla by pounding the ice. So she put the cubes into a plastic bag, grabbed the meat mallet from the drawer and darted outside to crush the ice into chips against the ground. Then she rushed back inside to bring them to Noah in a glass.

But the couch was empty and she spotted him in the hall, crawling toward the bathroom. After he came out, she helped him back to the sofa and sat in the armchair across from him so she could support him down the hall the next time he felt sick to his stomach. They must have made half a dozen trips back and forth before he finally fell asleep. Arleta smoothed back his dark, damp hair to place a hand on his bare forehead; he was still feverish, but not quite as hot as before.

No sooner did she drop into the armchair than she heard Sovilla's door open, so Arleta popped back up and repeated a similar process of assisting her back and forth between her bed and the bathroom. The older woman finally fell back asleep just as the sun was coming up. Arleta returned to the living room to steal a few minutes of rest in the armchair. Only then did it occur to her that her bare ankle was exposed, but before she could get up to put on her socks, she nodded off to sleep.

Noah opened his eyes and quickly shut them again. Then he reopened them just a crack, squinting as he looked around the living room. The sunlight seemed brighter than usual, and he wasn't sure if he was dreaming or not. He had hazy recollections of sipping water, eating crackers, using the bathroom or talking to Sovilla and Arleta at various times during the night, but he didn't know if any of it had actually happened.

But when Arleta came into his range of vision, he was certain she was real, not a dream, because he felt her cool hand on his forehead and heard her murmur, "I think your fever's gone."

He tried to ask how his grandmother was, but his throat was too scratchy to get the words out. Arleta supported his head and lifted a glass to his lips so he could take a sip of water. "Is *Groossmammi* okay?"

"*Jah*, she's doing very well. She's taking a nap in her room. She fared a lot better than you did. After the second day, she was almost as *gut* as new."

Noah tried to sit up but it made him dizzy so he rested against the pillow again. "The second day? How long have I been sleeping?"

"Off and on since *Muundaag*. It's *Freidaag* now."

"*Freidaag? Neh!*"

"*Jah*, it is. Feel your chin—you're growing quite the beard."

Noah touched his cheeks and chin; they were prickly with hair. "I don't remember so much time passing. I must have been really sick."

"You were. How do you feel now?"

"*Baremlich.*" Although most of the past week was a blur, one thing he recalled perfectly was what he'd said to Arleta when he'd found out Sovilla was ill. As terrible as he'd felt physically, he felt even more wretched for accusing her of not caring about his grandmother's health when clearly *he* was the one who'd brought home the flu.

"*Jah*, that makes sense. You'll probably be weak for several days." Arleta adjusted the pillow behind his head and then tucked the sheet around him. "What can I do to make you more comfortable?"

Noah clutched her fingers to get her attention. She stopped fussing with the bedding and tipped her head quizzically at him. "I don't feel *baremlich* because of the flu—well, I do, but I feel more *baremlich* about the things I said to you," he confessed. "I am very, very sorry, Arleta."

She pulled her fingers free of his grasp. "Don't wear yourself out talking about that now."

"*Neh*, this is important. Please listen." So she sat down in the armchair facing him. His voice crackling with dryness and emotion, he continued, "I was completely out of line. What I said was a reflection of my fear, not of your care for *Groossmammi*. I panicked because she's the only *familye* I have, and it's my responsibility to make sure…" Noah didn't usually feel so sentimental. Maybe it was that the virus was affecting his emotions, but his eyes welled and he couldn't complete the thought.

As Arleta leaned forward to help him take another sip of water, she assured him, "She's okay, Noah. She's fine. *Gott* kept her from becoming severely ill."

"*Jah.* But He used *you* to help her—to help both of us—recover. I can't say enough how grateful I am. Or how sorry I am. *I* was the one who brought the flu home to her, not you." Again, he was embarrassed when his vision blurred with tears.

"You don't know that for sure. You don't know where she got it."

"Maybe not, but I know she *didn't* get it from you. Please forgive me for accusing you of making her sick. Of not caring about her health," Noah pleaded.

"I *do* forgive you for that." Arleta set the water glass on the end table and then took a deep breath and said, "But there was something else you were wrong about, Noah. Your implication that I've behaved inappropriately with Isaiah in private was hurtful, untrue and ungentlemanly."

Noah had been so upset when he'd come home to discover Sovilla was ill that he'd said things he couldn't fully remember. But seeing the pain in Arleta's eyes and hearing the indignation in her voice brought the gist of his remarks back to him. "*Neh.* The implication I made was worse than that—it was *ungodly.* I am so ashamed, Arleta—and so sorry."

She bit her lip and nodded, but he could tell she was hesitant to accept his apology and he didn't blame her. Using all of his strength, he pushed himself up on one elbow. Grasping the back of the sofa with the other hand, he pulled himself the rest of the way up, until he was in a sitting position, directly facing her. The effort made him dizzy, and he rested his hands on his knees until they stopped trembling. Ordinarily, he never would have admitted what he was about to disclose—he could hardly admit it to himself—but he had to make Arleta believe he didn't really mean what he'd said.

"I—I made that remark—that horrible remark—because I wanted someone to blame for *groossmammi* being sick. And I blamed you and Isaiah because, well, because I've been envious of your courtship."

"Pah!" Arleta uttered. "Isaiah is *not* my suitor. I have no romantic interest in him whatsoever and I never did."

"Really? But you seem so enam—" He stopped talking before he put his foot in his mouth again.

Fortunately, Arleta giggled. "I seem so enamored of him, is that it? I suppose I can understand why you and our peers may have thought that. I *was* 'chasing him down' for a ride after the potluck. But that was only because I wanted to allow *you* the opportunity to give Hannah a ride home alone."

"Why would I want to do that?"

Arleta's cheeks flushed and she looked down at her lap. "You know, so you could renew your courtship with her."

Aha, that's *why she looks so guilty. Someone must have told her I used to be Hannah's suitor.* "I'm about as interested in a courtship with Hannah as you are with Isaiah."

Arleta lifted her head. "Really?"

"*Jah.* I can't see myself in a courtship with any-one. That's why I was envious of your courtship with Isaiah—because I know that a courtship isn't some-thing I can ever have." Whoa. Noah's fatigue must have dulled his inhibition because he'd come very close—*too* close—to confiding far more than he wanted to con-fide. He rubbed his forehead, hoping Arleta wouldn't pick up on what he'd just admitted, but it was too late.

"What's stopping you from having a courtship?"

"I don't know why I said that. I might still be fe-verish," Noah said with a laugh, but Arleta wasn't dis-tracted.

"If it's because of your obligations to Sovilla, there's no reason you can't care for your *groossmammi* and care about a *weibsmensch* at the same time, you know," Ar-leta said. "And I don't think anything would make So-villa happier than seeing you in a courtship."

"You don't have to tell *me* that," Noah said with a wry laugh. Dropping the subject, he asked, "Could you please help me up now?"

His legs were so weak that as soon as he got up, even though Arleta was holding on to him, he had to sit back down again. While he was resting before he gave it a second try, Sovilla entered the room.

"Noah, you're awake, my little *schlofkopp*!" She joy-fully called him a sleepyhead and then crossed the room to kiss his forehead before sitting down next to him. "How are you feeling?"

He glanced at Arleta, whose smile showed the small opening between her teeth—she'd completely forgiven him. "I feel *wunderbaar* now, relatively speaking. Except I can't wait to shave off this beard."

"Oh, but it gives me a glimpse of what you'll look like when you get married. I think he wears it well, don't you, Arleta?"

"*Jah*, he looks very handsome in it," she said, winking at Sovilla—or maybe at Noah. And he felt so invigorated by her compliment that he rose from the couch all by himself.

Of course, after making up with Noah, Arleta didn't leave New Hope. In fact, wild horses couldn't have dragged her away, especially now that she had *two* patients to attend to. Not that Sovilla was much of a patient; she was a little wobblier than usual, probably because she still wasn't eating enough, even though the nausea and stomach pain had long passed. But Noah was so weak he needed help just crossing the room, and he spent the next several days sleeping more hours than he was awake.

Fortunately, that week was an off-Sunday, so the trio was able to worship at home and after they'd prayed and read the Bible together, Sovilla went to her room to nap and Noah rested on the couch, as he still didn't have the strength to climb the stairs. Arleta sat opposite him, gazing at his face. The angles of his jaw and cheekbones were more pronounced, once he'd shaved off his beard. It occurred to her that she didn't realize he'd been slowly gaining weight since she'd been there until he got sick and lost it again. Still, she thought he looked as masculine as ever, although his physical traits were the least important of the attributes she found attractive about him.

No wonder Hannah wishes she had a second chance to have him as her suitor, she thought. As uncharitable as it was, she felt a small measure of satisfaction to discover Noah wasn't interested in courting her. *I'm sorry that it will hurt her feelings when she finds out, but I just can't see him with her. I never really could...*

"Are you sitting there watching me sleep?" Noah asked, opening one eye.

Caught, she joked, "*Neh*—because you're not actually sleeping. But I'll leave if I'm making you uncomfortable."

"You're not. I can't really sleep anyway." He slowly sat up and swung his feet around to the floor. "You know, when I was sick, I had the strangest dreams. In one of them, you weren't wearing socks."

Arleta's pulse quickened. "Do you remember anything else about that dream?"

"You mean like did you have hooves instead of feet?" He laughed. "Now that I think about it, I do remember something else. It was the oddest thing."

"What was that?" Arleta squeaked.

"You were holding a mallet."

Relieved, she cracked up and told him about going outside to crush the ice into chips for him so she wouldn't wake Sovilla by making such a loud noise in the house. She thought he'd find it amusing to picture her outside in the middle of the night pounding ice with a meat mallet, but instead he shook his head, frowning. "What's wrong?" she asked.

"*Me.* I'm wrong. I mean, I *was* wrong. So wrong. You've taken such *gut* care of *Groossmammi* and me, right down to the smallest detail and—"

"Noah," she interrupted him. "You apologized and I've forgiven you so there's no need to continue to feel sorry or to keep apologizing to me. Otherwise, it's as if you haven't accepted my forgiveness."

"Okay. *Denki*," he said. Then he sighed. "I don't think *Groossmammi* is going to let me go to work tomorrow. Not that she can really stop me, but I'd better prepare for an argument."

"*I'm* not going to let you go to work tomorrow—and I *can* stop you. I'll hitch the horse to the fence at the end of the lane if I have to," Arleta threatened. She was laughing, but she meant it. "You can hardly balance well enough to cross the living room floor. How do you expect to pull yourself up a ladder or walk on a rooftop?"

"*Jah*, I guess I can give it another day of rest."

Another week is what you'll need, Arleta thought, but she didn't say it aloud. There was no need for her to convince him; his body would show him his limitations.

Sure enough, over the next couple of days, Noah's strength began to return, but at a much slower pace than he wanted it to. By Thursday morning, he was chomping at the bit to return to work, but he still wasn't even capable of caring for the animals; Arleta had to do it. She didn't mind, but it frustrated Noah that she was single-handedly managing the household, livestock and yardwork and he couldn't help her.

"See what happens when you don't get enough rest for weeks on end? Along comes a virus and knocks you completely out of commission," Sovilla chided him. "You lectured me about my weak immune system, but I think yours was even more fragile."

Arleta noticed that after so many days of being housebound together without a break, Sovilla and Noah were getting on each other's nerves. "It's such a pretty day today. Noah, why don't we take a ride to the market together? I need flour because tomorrow Sovilla's going to teach me to make a bumbleberry pie. And maybe we can stop off at the lake you told me about. What's it called again?"

"It's a pond. Little Loon Pond. But I don't think it's a *gut* idea to leave *Groossmammi* alone for that long."

Sovilla harrumphed exaggeratedly. "And *Groossmammi* doesn't think it's a *gut* idea for *you* to *stay with her* for so long."

Arleta tried not to giggle. "We'll leave after lunch and we'll be home before supper. How does that sound?"

"Like just what the doctor ordered," Sovilla said.

Noah seemed less pleased than his grandmother was but once they were underway, his mood lightened considerably. Although Arleta had insisted on hitching the horse and buggy herself, Noah had taken the reins once she'd given him a boost into the buggy. She asked him to stop at the store first, so she could get her errand out of the way before they relaxed at the pond. "I'll only be in there a few minutes," she said, as she climbed down onto the pavement in front of the little market on Main

Street. He said he'd circle the block instead of hitching the horse in the back parking lot.

He hadn't returned yet when she came out of the store, so she stood in the shade of the awning. After a few minutes passed, she began to get worried. *Maybe I shouldn't have pushed him to* kumme *out*, she thought. But just then, his buggy rounded the corner and he pulled over by the sidewalk.

Climbing in, she asked, "Are you okay?"

"*Jah.* I wanted to get a treat for us to enjoy at the pond. You get to choose which one you want." He handed her a small paper bag.

Arleta peeked inside. The bag contained two plastic spoons and two small containers of homemade ice cream from the local ice cream parlor farther down Main Street. One was pink-colored and the other was clearly chocolate-flavored. She didn't even have to ask whether the pink was strawberry or peppermint; she wanted the chocolate. "What a sweet thing to do, especially since you had to hitch the horse and get in and out of the buggy by yourself."

"That's how I felt about you running outside to pound ice into chips for me," he said, his eyes fixed on her.

A delicious shiver rattled her shoulders, and Arleta broke eye contact with him and quickly set the bag on the seat between them. "The ice cream is making me cold already," she fibbed.

When they reached the pond, Noah turned down the dirt road that ran parallel with David Hilty's backyard. His coworker had cleared this path on his property specifically so his Amish district members could have easy access to the waterfront without cutting across his lawn and disturbing his family. After hitching the horse to the post David had erected, Noah slowly led Arleta through a short wooded path to a grassy clearing where two canoes lay overturned in front of the glassy water.

"Oh, look how beautiful the pond is—it's crystal clear. And it feels about ten degrees cooler here than in town," she marveled appreciatively.

"*Jah*. I like the gorge, too, but this is actually my favorite spot in all of New Hope."

"I can see why. Do you want to go out in a canoe or eat our ice cream here?"

Feeling a little winded, Noah suggested they should eat their ice cream first and canoe later. He helped Arleta spread the blanket she'd brought and they sat down, stretching their legs out in front of them. For a few minutes, they licked the creamy treat from their spoons, taking in the pristine scenery without talking. Soon, the tranquility of the setting—or maybe it was Arleta's soothing presence—made Noah realize how agitated he'd been earlier.

"I'm sorry if I've seemed cranky lately," he told her. "It's frustrating that I can't return to work yet."

"I understand. It can't be much *schpass* for you to be stuck in the *haus* with two *weibsleit* all day when you're used to being outdoors with your coworkers."

Actually being "stuck" indoors with Arleta had been the best part of his recovery. "*Neh*. That's not it. It's that I keep calculating how far behind I am financially, and there's absolutely nothing I can do about it. My body just isn't strong enough yet."

Arleta squinted at him, a pinched expression on her face. "You're struggling financially?"

Ach, had he actually said that aloud? Noah had only meant to assure Arleta it wasn't her company—it wasn't Sovilla's, either—that was making him cantankerous. But now that it had slipped out, there was no taking it back and he didn't want Arleta to mention his concern to Sovilla, so he clarified his statement. "I'm not struggling presently, *neh*... If I explain, do you promise not to tell my *groossmammi*?" When she nodded, he delved into the details of his plan to save enough money to take Sovilla to Mexico if it became necessary.

"Oh, so *that's* why you've been working so many hours!" she exclaimed.

"*Jah.* Why? Did you think it was because I'm greedy?"

"*Neh.* Not at all. I just figured it was because you were trying to keep up with customer demand," she said. "I should have known it had something to do with Sovilla—you're always so careful to put her needs first."

"It was *dumm* to work such long hours without taking enough breaks, though. *Groossmammi* was right—that's why the flu hit me so hard. Now I'm not sure if I'll ever catch up."

Arleta set her spoon in her empty cup and placed it at her side. "Listen, Noah. I've long felt that you've overcompensated me for staying with—"

"*Neh, neh, neh,*" he cut her off. "I didn't tell you about my concern so you'd offer to—"

Now *she* cut *him* off. "Wait, just hear me out, please.

I've felt guilty taking such a big salary for what feels like such a little bit of work. Especially now that Sovilla is doing so much better. I'd be *hallich* to work without pay for the rest of the summer—and I'd *still* feel as if I earned more money than I deserved."

Noah was adamant—it was *his* responsibility to take care of his family, and that included meeting their financial obligations. "I committed to paying you a certain salary, and I'm going to honor that commitment. I'll think of another solution if it becomes necessary to go to Mexico. But *denki* for your offer."

Arleta turned to face him, her eyes as vibrant green as the leafy branches overhead. "I respect your decision, Noah, but if you change your mind, my offer still stands. I'd do anything I could to help Sovilla if her cancer recurs. You know how fond I am of her."

Jah, but do you know how fond I am of you? Noah thought. He was about to reiterate his gratitude for her offer when Arleta swiveled her head and bent her knee to her chest, clutching her ankle.

"Ouch!" she screeched. "Something just bit me!"

Noticing a wasp crawling over her ice cream cup and aware that she often swelled up from insect bites and stings, Noah said, "I think you've been stung. Here, let me look."

"Neh," she yelped, hopping up off the blanket.

"Do you want me to ask the Hiltys if they have antihistamine?"

"Neh! I want you to give me some space!" she wailed and limped toward the water, tears streaming down her cheeks.

* * *

Although a burning pain coursed through Arleta's ankle, she wasn't crying because of the wasp sting. She was crying because for the past hour, she been allowing herself to *pretend* she was on a date. Which wasn't difficult to do, considering that Noah had bought her ice cream and confided an intimate secret to her and gazed at her with the same cherishing expression as he'd looked at the pond, his favorite place in all of New Hope. But then the wasp had stung her on the ankle, of all places, cruelly reminding her that she shouldn't be entertaining any notion of a courtship, not even a pretend one. *That's* why she was crying.

That, *and* because she was terrified that Noah would discover her secret. She hadn't meant to speak so harshly to him, but she didn't know how else to make him back off so she could unlace her shoe and examine her ankle. Even before she removed her footwear and peeled off her sock, she could tell how bad the swelling was because of how tight her skin felt. She took off her other shoe and sock and walked into the pond up to her shins. The chilly water alleviated her pain a little, but more importantly, as she stood there gazing toward the opposite shoreline, she was able to regulate her breathing. In turn, her heart rate, which had accelerated wildly from the release of histamine, also slowed.

When she finally turned around again, she spotted Noah standing beside the blanket, watching her. "Is that helping?"

"A little." As she began wading toward him, he moved in her direction, too. She quickly hurried out of the water and slapped mud over her ankle before he reached her. "I've read that when the mud dries, it can draw the wasp venom out. But I don't know if it's actually true."

"I guess it's worth a try."

"I'm sorry, but I don't think I can go canoeing now," she said, reaching to put her sock and shoe on her right foot.

"That's okay. I wouldn't have been able to paddle very far anyway. I'm beat. How about if we *kumme* back, let's say, a week from *Sunndaag* when I'm stronger?"

"I'd really like that," Arleta agreed. Noah picked up the blanket and empty ice cream containers, and Arleta retrieved her other sock and shoe. Then he extended his arm. "Is that so I can lean on you or so you can lean on me?"

He laughed. "A little of each."

So she took his arm and they hobbled down the path toward the buggy. *This might not have been a real date*, Arleta said to herself, *but I can't think of a more romantic way for it to end.*

Chapter Ten

To Arleta's disappointment, Noah returned to work the following Monday. They'd been getting along so well—in between Arleta's chores, they'd play spades with Sovilla or checkers with each other, read the Bible aloud or just chat. In the afternoons when Sovilla was napping, Arleta and Noah would take a stroll around the yard to build up his endurance and tolerance of the heat again. Those were the times Arleta liked best, mostly because she was alone with Noah, but also because he'd begun telling her stories about his family, which he hadn't done since he'd shared the anecdote about him and his brothers "skitching" when they were teenagers.

So after Mike picked him up on Monday morning, Arleta felt sulky and restless. She did the breakfast dishes and hung out the laundry and then went into the living room and plunked into a chair with a huff. "It's unbearably hot already and it's only nine o'clock," she complained to Sovilla. "I hope I sent enough meadow tea with Noah. I don't want him to get dehydrated."

"I'm sure he has plenty."

"*Jah*, but I should have packed more fruit for him. I should have cut his sandwich into quarters, too, so he could take several breaks instead of eating it all at once. That's not *gut* for his stomach."

"I thought you were supposed to be tending to *me*, not to him," Sovilla said.

"Oh!" Arleta sprang to her feet. "What can I do for you?"

"I was teasing, dear."

"You don't feel ill?"

"*Neh*. And I think when I have my tests done next Thursday, we'll find out I'm as fit as a fiddle."

Arleta had been so wrapped up in helping Noah recover that she'd completely forgotten about Sovilla's important appointment. "*Gott* willing, that's exactly what we'll find out. But maybe you should eat a handful of blueberries daily, just in case. I read an article that said blueberries contain something called antioxidants, which play a role in preventing cancer."

"Was that in the same book that suggested putting mud on a bee sting?" Sovilla asked. She had been incredulous the afternoon Arleta limped into the house with mud caked on her ankle. Fortunately, by the time Arleta was done showering, the swelling had subsided considerably and she'd put on a fresh pair of socks so neither Noah nor his grandmother ever caught a glimpse of her tattoo.

"*Neh*. I read about antioxidants in one of Noah's pamphlets in the kitchen drawer." Because she sensed Sovilla was still skeptical, she said, "But it didn't actually say the blueberries *would* prevent cancer, or how quickly they might work. Just that it's *gut* to include them in your daily diet."

"Do raspberries and strawberries contain these antioxidants, too?"

"*Jah.* Why?"

"Because I need to teach you how to make a bumbleberry pie before you leave New Hope."

Arleta was scheduled to go home about a week after Sovilla's follow-up doctor's appointment, which was when Sarah would be available to come over again, baby in tow, if the older woman still needed care. That meant Arleta had a little less than three weeks left in New Hope. On one hand, she looked forward to returning to Serenity Ridge because she missed her family so much. On the other hand, she knew she was going to miss Sovilla terribly, too. And she couldn't even allow herself to imagine about how sad she'd be when she left Noah.

Pushing the thoughts away, she tried to refocus on their conversation. What was it they'd just been talking about? Oh, yes, Sovilla was going to reveal her special recipe for bumbleberry pie. "I've heard that you have a secret."

She was referring to Sovilla's secret ingredient, but the older woman murmured, "Almost everyone has a secret, dear—which is a pity, since the majority of our secrets are shameful ones."

Clearly, she wasn't talking about ingredients, and Arleta's pulse raced like it had when she'd been stung by the wasp. Had Sovilla seen her tattoo the night Arleta hadn't been wearing socks and she'd helped the older woman back and forth down the hall? "What do you mean?"

"Oh, I suppose I'm just thinking aloud about how the more we try to keep the things we're ashamed of a secret, the more miserable we become. Shame has a way of robbing us of the abundant life—the *joy*—that Christ wants us to have."

Sovilla's words struck a chord with Arleta, and her mouth was so dry she could hardly speak. "But don't you think sometimes it's wiser to keep a secret to yourself than it is to share it…like if telling it could hurt someone else? Or if you know that someone is going to judge you unfairly for whatever it is you don't want them to know?"

"*Jah.* It's wise to exercise discretion depending on the circumstance and the people involved. But there's a big difference between keeping a secret to yourself and holding on to shame. If we've confessed a wrongdoing to the Lord, He's faithful to forgive us."

Recognizing the Bible passage Sovilla was referencing, Arleta interjected, "1 John 1:9 is one of my favorite verses."

"*Jah*, mine, too. I repeat it to myself frequently. The problem is, even though I believe *Gott* forgives me for my transgressions, sometimes I have a difficult time forgiving *myself.* I think a lot of people struggle with that tendency."

I know I *do*, Arleta thought, relieved to know she wasn't the only one.

Sovilla pushed herself up from the chair, exclaiming, "Just listen to me! You asked about my secret ingredient and instead I delivered a sermon. *Kumme*, let's go bake a pie before Noah returns home and I can't tear you away from the checkerboard again."

If it's that obvious to her how much I've been enjoying Noah's company, maybe it's obvious that I'm hiding something, too, Arleta thought as she followed Sovilla into the kitchen. *Maybe that's why she just said all of those things about secrets and shame?*

But even if she did suspect something, Arleta decided she wasn't going to worry about it. She only had a couple more weeks left in New Hope and as Sovilla indicated, it would be a pity if the secret shame of her tattoo robbed her of the joy she experienced in Noah's presence.

Not going to work may have felt frustrating to Noah, but *going* to work felt nearly futile. He'd work for half an hour, and then he'd need to rest for ten minutes. His hands weren't steady enough to set the screws at the proper tightness, and David had to check all of them. But worst of all, his concentration was lagging and he lapped a section of metal paneling the wrong way—a mistake not even Jacob made after his first week of training. Yet his coworkers never complained; in fact, they encouraged him to take more frequent breaks.

"If you try to get back up to speed too soon, you'll relapse," David warned. "We're meeting our deadlines, so no need to worry."

It was true; the crew had worked extra hours during Noah's two-week absence and were right on target to fulfill their contractual obligations. "I don't know how you've managed to do it, but I sure appreciate it."

David gestured toward Jacob, who was helping Mike carry more panels across the lawn. "If you can believe it, Jacob has really stepped up. Apparently, the *maedel* he's been courting hinted that she couldn't marry a *mann* who didn't have a stronger work ethic." He chuckled. "It's almost as if the two of you have switched roles. He's working till seven or eight at night, and you're out picnicking in the day."

"What? Who told you that?"

David gave him a sheepish look. "My wife saw you and Arleta down by the pond the other day."

"We weren't *picnicking*. My *groossmammi* wanted me to get out of the *haus* and Arleta needed to go to the store. We stopped at the pond and had a dish of ice cream. We weren't there more than an hour," Noah explained, abashed that his coworker may have thought he was being lazy.

But David indicated he thought just the opposite when he grinned and said, "That's too bad—maybe you'll get to stay longer next time." He handed Noah a caulking tube; caulking was one of the least strenuous tasks in installing metal roofing. "Listen, *suh*, you could spend the next month napping in a hammock if you needed to and no one here would utter a word of complaint or question your diligence."

"Denki," Noah replied. He was grateful for his coworkers' industriousness, and he knew David's sentiment was sincere. It was a huge relief not to have to worry about the business, but there was still the matter of his side projects to consider. Noah was skeptical about making it through a full day of work as it was, so he couldn't envision himself putting in additional hours in the early evening, too. At least, not this week.

That meant he'd be three weeks behind in meeting his financial goal; the week he'd been sick, the week he'd recovered and this week, when he was easing back into work. *How will I ever make up for the lost time?* he wondered. Being bedridden for the past couple of weeks had given him even more time to pray about his grandmother's health, and he hoped they'd hear she was cancer-free when she had her bloodwork and scans done the following week. But he still had to be prepared for the possibility they'd need to travel to Mexico. *Maybe by next week, I'll be strong enough to pick up my pace with my side projects*, he thought.

As he caulked the flashing around the roof vent, Noah's mind drifted to Arleta. He wondered what she was doing at home right now. Usually around this time, Sovilla would be napping and he and Arleta would be taking a stroll around the house. During those times, Noah often found himself reminiscing to Arleta about his family—that's how natural it felt to talk to her. Noah could tell her anything. Well, *almost* anything. He'd never tell her what he'd been doing the night of the fire, of course.

From there, his mind leaped to thoughts of Hannah and Isaiah. It was funny how both Noah and Arleta suspected each other of having a romantic interest in their peers. Yes, he'd once courted Hannah, but in retrospect he would describe his feelings for her as infatuation, not *love*. And Arleta had said she had no romantic interest whatsoever in Isaiah. *It just goes to show the* narrish *conclusions people can leap to*, he thought.

Then it struck him that after seeing them together by the pond, David Hilty's wife may have concluded they were courting. Noah trusted David to exercise discretion, but he didn't know his wife well enough to guess if she'd disclose her observation to anyone else or not. *What if* Groossmammi *caught wind of a rumor like that?* he asked himself. He was pretty sure he could anticipate her response: initially, she'd be delighted…and subsequently, she'd be crushed to find out it wasn't true. He'd never hear the end of it. Noah supposed the one way to avoid disappointing her was not to do anything to perpetuate the rumors. In other words, he should tell Arleta he changed his mind about going to the pond again.

He *should*. But that didn't mean he wanted to. *Arleta's only going to be here for a few more weeks*, he thought. *Why should I give up spending time with her—which I really enjoy—just to spare my* Groossmammi *from disappointment? I shouldn't be penalized just because* she *chooses to believe rumors.*

For the rest of the afternoon, Noah wrestled with his conscience, unsure about whether he should cancel his outing with Arleta or not. But when he returned home and ambled up the walkway, he spied a bumbleberry pie cooling on the porch railing. Arleta sat in the glider nearby, flipping through one of her recipe books from the library. When she looked up, she gave him such an affectionate smile it literally put a hop in his step and as he bounced up the stairs, he knew exactly what he was going to do.

Arleta never would have *wished* Noah's weakness on him, but she couldn't deny how happy she was that it kept him home in the evenings instead of out working on extra installation projects. It was agonizing enough to be separated from him during the day. By late afternoon, her eagerness to see him again was so irrepressible that she'd have to wait on the porch, so Sovilla wouldn't notice how many times she glanced at the clock.

I think I'm falling in love with him and he's falling in love with me, too, she imagined writing to Leanna. She never did, of course. Instead, she sat with a blank tablet on her lap, unable to pick up her pen. She knew what she really ought to write was a letter to her parents, urging them to prohibit her sister from working for an *Englischer* family. But thinking about writing *that* letter reminded her of her tattoo, which in turn made her have to face how unrealistic it was to harbor daydreams about falling in love with Noah. And she cherished that reverie too much to give it up, at least until she had to leave New Hope.

Meanwhile, the only thing she anticipated more than his daily return home was their expedition to the pond on Sunday. So, after they returned home from church and Sovilla said she had an upset stomach and needed to nap, Arleta squeezed her fingers into fists behind her back to keep herself from crying. Noah was in the barn, giving the horse fresh water, but she knew as soon as he learned his grandmother was sick, he'd cancel their trip to the pond so they could stay home and keep an eye on her. Arleta agreed that was the prudent thing to do, but after spending the week imagining canoeing across the picturesque pond with him, staying home and playing spades while Sovilla snored in the next room didn't seem nearly as romantic.

Fortunately, she had underestimated Sovilla's bossiness. "Why would you stay here on a beautiful day like this?" she scoffed. "It's not as if you're going to watch me sleep."

"*Neh*, but we'll be here for you if you need help," Noah said.

"You can help me by taking the last of that bumbleberry pie with you so I won't eat it," Sovilla said. "That's the third one Arleta has made this week, and they've been so tasty that I've made a glutton of myself. Which is the only reason my stomach is upset."

"Okay," Noah agreed. "We won't be gone long, *Groossmammi*."

"Whether you're gone five minutes or five hours

won't make much difference to me—I'm going to settle in for a long nap," she said.

"I hope she's really all right," Noah said as they pulled out onto the main road a few minutes later.

"If you feel uncomfortable leaving her, we can go back. She's probably asleep by now so she won't shoo us away again," Arleta reluctantly suggested.

Noah glanced over at her. "I was actually hoping you'd assure me she'll be fine, not suggest we go back."

Delighted that he still wanted to go to the pond as much as she did, Arleta replied, "I think she *will* be fine. But how about if we pray for her?" Noah nodded so as he guided the horse toward the pond, Arleta prayed that Sovilla's stomach pain would subside, she'd have a refreshing rest and that the Lord would put Noah's mind at ease.

By the time they arrived at the pond, he was smiling broadly and Arleta was practically singing with glee as she commented about what a cool, sunny day it was and how much she hoped at least one of the canoes would be available for their use. When they got to the pond, they were pleased to see both canoes overturned onshore. Flipping one of them over, they found two life vests, but only a single paddle stashed beneath it. Which was fine with Arleta—it meant instead of keeping her back toward Noah as she helped paddle, she'd be able to face Noah during their excursion.

He quickly unlaced his boots, took off his socks and rolled up his pant legs. Arleta had been so excited about their trip that she'd forgotten to come up with an excuse about why she had to leave her footwear on.

Fortunately, when Noah noticed she wasn't taking

her shoes off, he asked, "Are you afraid you'll get stung on your ankles again?"

"*Jah*. It was *lappich* of me to forget to bring an antihistamine."

"I'd better help you in, then," he said. Since half of the canoe was still on dry land, she easily stepped inside without getting her feet wet. Then Noah held her hand for balance as she inched toward the seat at the far end. He set the insulated bag containing their pie and water bottles in the middle of the vessel and then pushed off shore and hopped in. He paddled with such long, determined strokes that she never would have guessed at how ill he'd been the week before.

"I want to take you to the other side to show you something really pretty."

"It's *all* really pretty," she raved. The pond was encircled by gentle hills comprised of tall pines and leafy oaks and maples. Large, rounded rocks protruded in clusters at various spots along the shoreline, which was typical in that part of Maine. The water was so clear and still she could see to the bottom if she peered over the side; up in the distance, the trees were mirror images of themselves on the water's surface. "It's like we're rowing through the hills!" she exclaimed, enchanted.

But Noah was right; the alcove he brought her to was even prettier, like a pond within a pond. Shaded by nearby maple trees, the little circle of water was dappled with sunlight that danced with the breeze. To their right, cobalt blue damselflies darted between pink water lilies with orange centers; to the left, a torrent of water cascaded over a graduated bank of rocks on shore. The sight of the waterfall was rivaled only by its sound and Arleta closed her eyes. "Listen to that," she murmured.

"If you like how it sounds and looks, you'll love how it feels. I don't think we'll run into any bees over there—you want to go dip your feet in?"

Arleta opened her eyes to see Noah looking expectantly at her. She hated to disappoint him when he was so eager to share an experience that he treasured with her, but there was no way she could remove her socks. "I'd like to, but I'm actually a little chilly."

"Jah," he said agreeably, looking toward the sky. "Today feels more like autumn than like summer."

Reluctant to acknowledge that August was already here—today was August 2—Arleta reminded him, "Summer's not over yet. We'll still have plenty more hot days. It would be more refreshing to stick our feet in if the weather's warmer." *And maybe by then I could think of an excuse to cover my tattoo with a bandage ahead of time.* It was a foolish idea, but if it meant she could come back here with Noah, Arleta would have risked giving it a try.

"Jah. We probably shouldn't stay too long here today anyway," Noah said. "But I think we've got time to eat some of that pie you packed, don't you?"

Unfortunately, he'd set the insulated bag in the middle of the canoe, too far out of reach for either of them to retrieve it. So Noah very carefully stood and climbed over the seat until the bag was within his grasp. He gave it to Arleta and then sat down knee-to-knee with her. They had to eat the pie with their hands since Arleta had forgotten to pack forks, but afterward they dipped their fingers in the water to wash them.

Then Arleta unzipped the bag, removed a bottle of water and leaned forward, extending it to him. "You must be thirsty after all that paddling."

Her eyes were glistening, and the sunlight sparkling across the surface of the water illuminated her face from beneath. Once again, just as on the day she arrived in New Hope, Noah had the feeling he knew her from somewhere else.

Then it struck him: he *had* seen her at the house building six years ago after all. *She's the one who brought me a glass of lemonade when I was hiding in* Daed's *workshop.* Noah recalled how he'd felt that day. Even though he'd known his church family and members of the surrounding Amish communities were rebuilding his house as a demonstration of their love and care for Sovilla and him, he had felt so undeserving that he couldn't face them. And he may have been imagining it, but it seemed to him that they averted their eyes whenever they passed him, too, as if they knew how miserably he'd failed his family and couldn't stand the sight of him.

But Arleta, Arleta had broken through his isolation and dejection by seeking him out and bringing him a glass of lemonade. By looking *into* his eyes, instead of away...

A breeze blew her *kapp* string across her cheek and without thinking, Noah lifted his hand to brush it away. "Such a lovely face, how could I ever forget it?" he murmured to himself.

Except he hadn't murmured to himself; apparently he'd said it *aloud*, because Arleta replied, *"Denki,"* and then sat straight again, holding his gaze.

He supposed he should have felt embarrassed or rushed to explain that he'd been thinking about where he'd met her before. But Arleta didn't seem at all flustered by his remark and he wasn't sorry for saying it, so he couldn't apologize. After a few seconds, she glanced down to unscrew the top of her water bottle and he did the same with his. And as he lifted it to his lips and swallowed, he thought about how the only time any drink ever tasted better was the day she'd brought him the lemonade.

"We should get back now," he said when his bottle was empty.

"Jah," she agreed. "Or else Sovilla will worry about us instead of the other way around, for a change."

He chuckled in agreement but he paddled back slowly and then walked to the buggy even slower, not wanting this feeling, or his time alone with Arleta, to end. *Maybe it doesn't have to,* he reflected as the horse pulled the carriage down the final road leading to his home. *Maybe the Lord has brought her into my life again for a reason. It could be that—*

"Ambulance!" Arleta pointed with one hand and grabbed Noah's arm with the other, jarring him from his thoughts.

He had been so preoccupied he hadn't registered that the emergency vehicle was barreling in his direction. Noah managed to bring the buggy to a halt and keep the horse settled as the vehicle whizzed by, its lights flashing and sirens screaming. There were two other houses on this long, flat country road, both belonging to *Englischers,* and if Sovilla *had* actually had an emergency, she wouldn't have been able to summon an ambulance since she didn't have a phone. But Noah was immediately gripped by fear. *Something's happened to*

Groossmammi *and I wasn't here to help her! I was out flirting with a* maedel, *just like on the night of the fire.*

He urged the horse into a quick canter, despite Arleta's protests, only slowing the animal to a trot when they reached the private lane where Noah's house was located. Even so, they took the turn at such a fast clip it seemed the carriage came precariously close to tipping. Instead of veering off toward the barn where the dirt driveway forked, Noah brought the animal to a halt in front of the house. Without a word to Arleta, he jumped down and bolted up the porch steps and into the kitchen. *"Groossmammi!"* he shouted upon finding it empty. *"Groossmammi!"* He rushed into the living room just as Sovilla flew in from the opposite entryway, wide-eyed, her hand on her heart.

"What is it? What's wrong? Did something happen to Arleta?"

"Neh." He embraced his grandmother so tightly against his chest that her headscarf went crooked. "I—I—I saw an ambulance and I—I thought something happened to you," he said, gasping in between words.

Sovilla patted his back. "Hush, now. Hush. I'm okay. Nothing happened." Noah's grandmother stood in the middle of the floor, holding him in her arms and humming, the way she might have comforted a baby, which seemed fitting because Noah was crying like one.

After a few minutes, he quieted but didn't pull away from her embrace until he heard footsteps on the porch; Arleta must have returned from stabling the horse.

"Please don't tell Arleta," he implored quietly, backing toward the hall. Sovilla seemed to understand he meant he didn't want Arleta to know that he'd overreacted, or why.

A minute later, as he stood over the sink in the bathroom, he heard Arleta ask, "Is Noah okay? All of a sudden he rushed home so quickly, I didn't know what was wrong."

"He's not feeling quite himself—he dashed into the bathroom."

"Oh, that's too bad. We'd had such a pleasant afternoon, but maybe he overdid it. Next time, we should go on a shorter outing."

There won't be a next time, Noah thought as he splashed cold water on his face. *Twice was two times too many.*

Arleta didn't understand it. On Sunday at the pond, Noah had told her she had a lovely face. A face he could never forget. But in the three days since then, unless she initiated a conversation, he hardly spoke a word to her. *Maybe it's just that he's exhausted from taking on too much too soon*, she surmised on Wednesday evening. After all, he was back to the same schedule he'd followed before he got sick; working all day, returning home to have a few bites of supper and then heading out to work on additional side projects until dark.

"Do you think Noah's okay?" she asked Sovilla. For the third night in a row, he'd gone straight to bed when he returned from his second job, even though it wasn't yet nine o'clock.

"He's probably just tired—he's still recovering, dear."

"*Jah*, but he seems…downhearted or something."

"Perhaps he's worried about what the doctor will tell me tomorrow."

Of course—that's it. I shouldn't have been so self-centered to think he's been distancing himself from me on purpose, Arleta thought.

As she lay in bed that night, she prayed for Sovilla's healing, just as she'd been praying ever since she came to New Hope, as well as for Noah's peace of mind. The only other thing Arleta could think of doing that might be helpful was to remind him that she was willing to forfeit her salary if it turned out his grandmother needed additional medical care. She decided she'd talk to him before he left for work in the morning. But when she woke, it was Sovilla who was drinking coffee alone in the kitchen.

"Guder mariye," she greeted her. "Is Noah up yet?"

"Jah, he left extra early, since he's coming home at noon to accompany me to my appointment."

"What time is the driver arriving?"

"Eleven forty-five."

"Then we won't have time to eat lunch before we go. I'll make sandwiches for us to eat on the way," Arleta offered.

"I'd appreciate that, dear, but I think it's best if Noah and I go alone to this appointment. It's…it's a *familye* thing, you see," Sovilla said, apologetically squeezing Arleta's hand.

"Jah, of course. I completely understand." She plastered a smile on her face and kept it there for the rest of the morning. But after Noah came home and the driver picked them up and she stood on the porch waving, Arleta ran into her room and bawled into her pillow. *It serves me right to be so disappointed*, she thought, feeling much the same way she felt after Ian broke up with her. *That's what I get for imagining I'm more special to someone than I actually am.*

Chapter Eleven

Noah paced on the sidewalk in front of the medical center in Portland. A nurse had just told him Sovilla had finished meeting with the doctor and offered him the use of a phone so he could arrange for their ride home. But then his grandmother had been delayed in coming out, so Noah had gone outside to ask the driver to wait a little longer. Apparently, their ride hadn't arrived yet, either.

As he strolled up and down the concrete, alternately scanning the exit for Sovilla and the parking lot for their van, he prayed, *Please,* Gott, *give me the strength to accept it if my* groossmammi *has cancer again. And please provide me a way to help her get additional care.*

He pressed a hand to his abdomen. Ever since he'd spotted the ambulance tearing down the road by his house, he'd had a knot in his stomach. It eased up a little after he'd discovered that no harm had befallen his grandmother, but right now, it was so tight that his discomfort rivaled the pain he'd experienced when he came down with the flu.

At least Arleta's not here, he thought, grateful that

Sovilla hadn't invited her to accompany them to this appointment, as he feared she would. Noah wouldn't have wanted Arleta to see him in this state, nor would he have wanted to be alone with her while Sovilla was getting her scans and consulting with her oncologist. It had been awkward enough to be in her company when the three of them ate supper at night. He was counting down the days until she left New Hope, and he wouldn't have a constant reminder that once again, he'd put his own pleasure above his family's safety. The fact that his grandmother *hadn't* actually had an emergency was irrelevant; he still felt ashamed and irresponsible.

"Noah!" Sovilla flagged him down as she emerged from the revolving door, tears in her eyes.

Oh, neh. *Please,* Gott, *give me strength*, he requested again as he strode toward her to take her arm. "What did the *dokder* say?"

"It's gone. The cancer is all gone," she told him.

"That's *wunderbaar, Groossmammi!*" Noah squeezed her hand, trying to be discreet in public. But the expression on his face must have shown his elation, because an elderly *Englisch* couple passing by smiled at them.

"Good news?" the white-haired lady asked.

"The best," he said.

"Praise God for that," the man remarked.

Which was exactly what Noah was already doing, silently praying, Denki, *Lord*, as he helped Sovilla into the silver minivan that had pulled up in front of them.

On the return trip, he and Sovilla sat side by side in the back seat, quietly watching the scenery go by. Noah continued to rejoice inwardly about his grandmother's health, and he assumed she was thinking similar thoughts. It wasn't until they were almost home that she spoke to him, using their *Pennsylfaanisch Deitsch* dialect so the driver couldn't understand them.

"I don't know why the Lord has blessed me with a second chance—with *continued* life," she said. "Especially when your *schweschder* and *brieder* and *eldre*'s lives were so short in comparison."

Noah swallowed. They'd just gotten such joyful news; why was his grandmother reminding them of something so sorrowful now? "*Groossmammi*, please," he pleaded, but she ignored him.

"For the longest time, I wished *I* had been the one who died in that fire, instead of them. I didn't understand why the Lord took young *kinner* home instead of an old *weibsmensch* like me. And I blamed myself for going to Ohio to visit my *schweschder.* I thought if I had been here, I could have prevented the fire since I was always more vigilant about the lamps than anyone else was."

"It wasn't your fault," Noah objected. *It was mine.*

"I know that now. But for some months afterward, I felt guilty and selfish because, quite frankly, I had been so delighted to get away to my *schweschder*'s *haus.* I missed her so much and she doesn't have any *kinskinner* living with her and…it was something pleasant I looked forward to each year," Sovilla confided. She paused, allowing Noah to absorb what she was telling him. "But ultimately, I trusted that my *suh*'s life—your *familye*'s lives—were in *Gott*'s hands, not mine. And that I wasn't at fault for enjoying the time I spent with my sister. But that I *would* be at fault if I didn't appreciate and accept the blessings the Lord gave me in the years following your *familye*'s deaths."

Noah never knew his grandmother had struggled with feelings so similar to his own. When she described how she'd thought it was her fault that his family had died, he recognized how misplaced her guilt was. Was it possible his guilt was misplaced, too? He turned his head to the side, blinking away a single tear.

Sovilla patted his knee. "You've taken excellent care of me, Noah, but when the Lord calls me home, I'm going, regardless." She chuckled. "But for today, I'm going to thank Him for the *gut* news and celebrate by enjoying a slice of bumbleberry pie when I get home. In addition to praising the Lord, what else are you going to celebrate?"

He shrugged. "I don't know."

"I'll make a suggestion," she said bluntly. "Arleta is worried about you, and I think she's hurt by your recent behavior toward her. Take her out for pizza."

Noah could tell by her tone that her suggestion wasn't really a suggestion; it was more or less an order. Besides, he really did want to speak to Arleta. So, after they'd returned home and shared the wonderful news with Arleta, and after she'd burst into tears and embraced Sovilla, Noah invited her to go into town for supper with him. She seemed to hesitate before accepting, which made sense, given how standoffish Noah had behaved toward her recently. But by the time the server brought their pizza to the table, they were talking and laughing as easily as ever.

"You're not eating much," Arleta said as she reached

for her third slice and he hadn't even finished his first. "Is your stomach bothering you?"

"*Jah*. But it's not from having the flu. I'm nervous because there's something I need to talk to you about," he admitted, setting his fork aside. Arleta put her pizza down on her plate, too. Noah took a swallow of water before continuing. "I am so grateful for your help during *groossmammi*'s recovery, as well as during mine, after I had the flu. I knew early on that the Lord was blessing us with your presence as a caregiver. And over time, I realized that He was blessing me with your friendship, too. And now I wonder if…if it's possible that He might want to bless me—hopefully, to bless *both* of us—by allowing me to become your suitor. I care about you deeply, Arleta, and it would be my privilege if I could demonstrate my affection and regard for you within the context of a courtship." Noah held his breath.

Arleta's lips parted and she blinked at him in surprise. "I'm very flattered that you'd ask to be my suitor," she said, and his heart plummeted. "But courtship often leads to marriage and I can't even consider that… I—I—I mean, I'm only twenty and…"

"There's no pressure or expectation about marriage. If we get to a point when we're serious about taking a step in that direction, we can talk about that then. But right now, my intention would be for us to get to know each other better, that's all." Noah added earnestly, "Even if we only courted for a couple of weeks, I'd consider it time well spent."

Arleta's mouth widened into a smile. Her eyes shone and she nodded. "In that case, I'd be *hallich* to have you as my suitor, Noah."

* * *

Arleta lay in bed, hugging her pillow. She was overjoyed about Sovilla's clean bill of health and thrilled that Noah had asked to be her suitor. Even the knowledge that she'd eventually have to break off their courtship didn't keep her from grinning. *I won't let it get out of hand*, she told herself. *I'll just enjoy having him as my suitor until next Saturday, when I return home. And maybe we'll exchange letters for a month or two after that. Then I'll end it, just like I did with Stephen, by saying it's too difficult to keep up a long-distance courtship.*

After all, this might be the only chance she had to have a suitor. And where was the harm in a little romance, provided she kept it light? Noah already expressed his feelings of affection for her; it would have been too awkward to turn him down and then continue to live in the same house with him. So she'd actually been *sparing* his feelings to accept him as her suitor. Besides, he'd said there was no pressure and he'd be happy to court her for even a few weeks.

On and on her rationalizations went. For every qualm she had about saying yes to Noah, she had two excuses to justify her decision. *I'll only be in New Hope until next Saturday, and I intend to soak up every last minute of my time with Noah*, she thought, as she rolled over and drifted off.

In the morning, she overslept, not rising until she heard Noah's footsteps on the porch as he returned from milking the cow. Arleta dressed quickly and went into the kitchen where he was sitting at the table and Sovilla was pulling a batch of muffins from the oven. "You shouldn't be doing that," Arleta chastised her after saying good morning.

"Why not? Haven't you heard? I'm cured," Sovilla jested wryly. "No more mollycoddling for me. It's time I start pulling my weight around here again."

"But making breakfast is *my* job," Arleta objected. "I wanted to fix breakfast scramble for Noah."

At the same time, Noah exclaimed, "Arleta can't leave yet!"

"My, my." Sovilla smirked, obviously amused by their outbursts. If she hadn't already guessed it, there couldn't have been any doubt in the older woman's mind now that the two of them were courting. "I'm not taking away your job, Arleta, and I'm not sending her home early, Noah. I just had a craving for muffins, that's all."

After that, they could hardly make eye contact with each other. Noah's cheeks stayed pink throughout the meal, and Arleta was so flustered she flipped a serving spoon out of the dish, sending bits of scrambled egg flying everywhere. Now that they were courting, she felt self-conscious interacting with him beneath Sovilla's watchful eye. And she was almost relieved when Noah returned from work that evening and announced that he had to dash out the door almost immediately after supper to work on the installment he'd started earlier in the week.

Before leaving, he sidled up to Arleta as she stood at the sink, washing dishes. "I probably won't complete the project until tomorrow," he whispered into her ear. "But there's no need for me to take on any new jobs next week. And we can go out alone together on *Sunndaag*."

"To the pond?" If so, Arleta was going to have to

think of an excuse to bandage her ankle in case he wanted to get out of the canoe by the waterfall.

"Neh," Noah replied. "Jacob said he and Faith plan to use the canoe. I thought we'd go back to the gorge. There's another trail I want to show you there."

"What will we tell your *groossmammi*?" Arleta whispered. Although they'd never blinked at telling Sovilla where they were going together in the past, now that they were actually courting, it seemed important for them to be more discreet about their outings.

"I don't know. I'll think of something," Noah promised.

But as it turned out, shortly after they'd had their home worship services and finished their lunch on Sunday, Lovina stopped by to pick up Sovilla and take her to the Stolls' house for a visit with Almeda. "Are you going canoeing today, too?" she asked Arleta.

"I'm sorry?"

"Honor said some of the *meed* are going canoeing. Faith and Hannah, I believe. Some of the *buwe* your age, too. I thought you'd be going with them."

"Neh, not today," Arleta said. *They didn't invite me. But that's okay—I'd rather go out with Noah, anyway.*

After Lovina and Sovilla left, Noah went to hitch the horse and Arleta put drinks and snacks into a thermal bag. As she stepped onto the porch, she noticed a buggy had pulled up in front of the house. Hannah Miller got out, carrying a container in each hand.

They exchanged greetings as she climbed the steps. "I brought you raspberries I picked from our patch. I thought you might want to use them when you make bumbleberry pie."

"*Denki*. Sovilla will be *hallich* to have fresh fruit," Arleta said, even though the trio had agreed they'd had their fill of bumbleberry pie for a while. She set the fruit inside the doorway and when she turned around, she noticed Hannah had taken a seat in the glider, as if she intended to stay. "Sovilla's not here," she informed her.

"That's okay, I didn't *kumme* to see her." Hannah blushed and glanced down at her feet, as if she were embarrassed. Had she come to see *Noah*? To ask him to go canoeing with the others? Arleta wondered. If she had, it seemed an even bolder gesture than when Arleta asked Isaiah for a ride, but before she could question her, Hannah said, "I came because there's something I need to say to you."

Arleta took a seat, too. She hoped whatever Hannah had to say, she'd say it quickly because she didn't want to waste even a moment of her time alone with Noah. *"Jah?"*

"I—I wanted to apologize for how I've treated you—for being so unfriendly," she said, hugging her arms to her chest as if she were cold. "I was jealous because I thought Isaiah was interested in you. That he wanted to court you. See, he used to be my suitor and we broke up a long time ago…anyway, I won't bother you with the details about that because it looks like you're on your way out. I just wanted you to know how sorry I am for how I acted, and I hope you'll forgive me."

Arleta couldn't contain her mirth—Hannah had never been interested in *Noah*; she was interested in *Isaiah!*—and she giggled. *"Jah*. Of course I forgive you."

Hannah lowered her brow. "Then what's *voll schpass*?"

"I'm laughing because Isaiah thought I was interested in him, too. And I don't blame him—especially not after I asked him for a ride home from the potluck. But I only did that because I was trying to give you and Noah the opportunity to ride home together. I sensed you were…not pleased with me and I figured it was because you thought I was interfering with a potential courtship between you and Noah."

"Noah and me? *Neh.* I couldn't ever see myself with him. Granted, we courted briefly when we were younger, but it was more of a crush than a serious courtship. Besides, he broke up with me and since then, we've hardly spoken."

Noticing the quaver in Hannah's voice, Arleta asked, "But that hurt your feelings, *jah*?"

"*Jah.* Not because I thought we had a future together, but because…well, because I always felt like he always kind of blamed me for his *familye*'s deaths. Or at least, that's what he associated me with."

"You? What did *you* have to do with the fire?"

Hannah met her eyes. "You won't tell anyone?"

"*Neh.* Not a soul," Arleta gravely replied.

"The night it happened we'd gone out on a date and afterward, we came back to my *haus* and were sitting on my porch. Noah should have dropped me off and then left because it was getting late, but we were sharing our first kiss and…anyway, by the time he got home, his family had perished. After that, he immediately broke off our courtship. I understood, because he was grieving at the time. But for years, he wouldn't even look at me. I felt like he blamed me."

"Oh, Hannah, that's *baremlich*." *It wasn't her fault—it wasn't Noah's fault, either, but I can understand why he may have felt like it was.* That *must be why he never allowed himself to court anyone after that...*

"Jah." Hannah picked at her thumbnail. "Like I've said, ever since then, we've hardly spoken but recently—in fact, it was that day I brought a pie over to your buggy after *kurrich*—something between us changed for the better. Like he'd forgiven me or something. And I wish him all the best. I truly hope one day he meets someone he wants to court, but I'd never consider him for myself as a suitor again." She stood up. "Anyway, I'd better get going. *Denki* for listening to what I had to say and for forgiving me, Arleta. I feel a lot better now."

"You're *wilkom*," she answered, even though *she* felt a lot worse. *Sovilla had said Noah hasn't courted anyone since he'd courted Hannah—which means he must really* like me. *After all he's been through, how can I toy with his feelings, knowing our relationship can never progress?* It was one thing to deceive herself, but to deceive Noah, when he was making himself so vulnerable after years of closing himself off, was absolutely disgraceful. Arleta had been selfish to accept his proposal of courtship, and she cared about him too much to toy with his feelings.

Dear Gott, she prayed. *Please forgive me. And please help Noah forgive me and accept my change of heart, too.*

Noah leaned against the side of the house, stupefied. He had been on his way to hitch the horse when he realized he'd forgotten his hat, so he'd turned around to get it. That's when he overheard Hannah talking to Arleta on the porch. Telling her that he and Hannah had been kissing the night of the fire. That *he*, essentially, was the one to blame for his family's deaths because he hadn't gone home when he should have. "That's *baremlich*," she had replied, but Noah didn't know exactly how to take her remark. Was it uttered in disbelief? Disgust? Or was it an expression of sympathy?

As appalled as Noah was that Hannah had told Arleta his shameful secret, in a way he was also relieved that she knew now, before their courtship progressed and he fell deeper in love with her than he already was. *What she does next will show me what she truly thinks of me*, he realized. *It will show me if it really is possible that the Lord wants to bless me with a wife and a fami-lye. Or at least, with a courtship that has the potential to lead to marriage.*

"Noah," Arleta called to him as she came around the corner. "What are you doing there?"

"I forgot my *hut*. I'll be right out. You can get in the buggy." He jogged into the house and returned a few seconds later. They traveled a good three miles in silence until, unable to stand the suspense any longer, he prompted, "You're awfully quiet. Is there something on your mind?"

"*Jah.* Could we pull over up there? I need to get out for a minute."

Noah's hands trembled as he held the reins, guiding the horse off the main road, stopping on a wide dirt shoulder. He followed Arleta when she got down and walked a few yards into the nearby meadow of tall grass and late summer wildflowers. She plucked a black-eyed Susan and twirled its stem between her fingers before turning around and saying, "I'm sorry, Noah, but I don't think I can be in a courtship with you."

He had sensed this was coming, but her decision still made his knees go weak. "Why not?"

"I just… It's like I said, I'm only twenty and I'm not really ready for a courtship."

"That's not the real reason, Arleta, is it?" he challenged. "You don't want to be in a courtship with me because of what Hannah Miller told you about—" He couldn't bring himself to say the words even now. "About me. I heard her talking to you so don't deny it."

Arleta's eyes were brimming. "I don't deny that she told me about the night of the fire, Noah, but that wasn't your fault. And it doesn't change the way I think of you at all, not one bit. I think you're the most thoughtful, responsible, devoted young *mann* I've ever met. And I think you're going to make a *wunderbaar* husband for some woman one day."

"If you really believe all of that, why don't you want me for your suitor?"

Arleta backed away, crying. "I'm sorry, but I can't tell you that. I just can't." Then she spun around and ran across the meadow and down the hill.

Some blessing a relationship with her turned out to be, Noah thought bitterly as he watched her disappear into the woods to take the shortcut home. *I wish she'd keep running all the way back to Serenity Ridge.*

Then, since he didn't want to have to be at the house alone with her, he climbed into the buggy and continued toward the gorge, where he spent the rest of the afternoon hiking. When the sun dropped low in the sky, he figured he had missed supper, which was what he intended, and he headed home.

"Did you have a nice time?" Sovilla asked when he stuck his head in the living room to say hello.

"Mmm. I'm beat—I'm going to go read for a while," he muttered, eager to get upstairs without bumping into Arleta. "Then I'll probably go to sleep. I've got a long week ahead of me—I'm going to be working in the evenings again." He had decided this was the perfect solution for avoiding Arleta.

His grandmother pressed her lips together and shook her head, but instead of scolding him, she said, "I'm *hallich* I'll have Arleta's company for another week—and for this evening. Where is she?"

"She's not here?"

"Neh."

Noah's first thought was that she'd arranged for a ride back to Serenity Ridge. He strode down the hall and rapped on her door. When there was no answer, he pushed it open; her Bible was still on the nightstand and her hairbrush was on the dresser. "She must have gotten lost in the woods again," he told his grandmother, grabbing the flashlight from its hook.

"So she wasn't with you today?"

"We—we got separated." Noah didn't take the time to explain further. As he hurried back toward the meadow where he'd dropped her off, he felt a mix of apprehension and resentment. *She's probably fine. For all I know, she emerged from the wrong side of the woods again and she's eating supper with the Wittmers,* he thought, tromping through the tall grass. Alternately, he worried. *What if she crosses paths with a wild animal?* There had been moose in the area and it was almost dusk, which was when they usually came out into the open.

"Arleta!" he shouted once he'd reached the woods. "Arleta!"

The farther he walked without seeing any sign of her, the harder his heartbeat drummed in his ears. His neck and back broke out in a sweat, and his familiar fears overtook him as he recalled what his grandmother had said after she found out that Isaiah had carried Arleta across the stream. "You ought to be more responsible, Noah. She's our guest."

Since he didn't know what direction she'd taken and had to scan the entire area carefully, Noah had to resist the urge to break into a run. "Arleta!" he yelled frantically. "Arleta, where are you?"

Although the sky was still bright, the woods were dense and dark. Noah turned on his flashlight and swept the beam from tree trunk to rock to tree trunk in front of him. "Arleta!" he shouted.

"Here I am," she wailed. "I'm over here!"

Noah rushed in the direction of her voice, stopping just short of a shallow but steep and rocky ditch. He could tell from her tone she was injured, and he lowered himself down beside her. "Where are you hurt?"

"My ankle. I can't walk," she sobbed. "I think it's broken."

He handed her the flashlight to distract her from the

pain. "You shine this on our path, okay? On the count of three, I'm going to pick you up." She moaned and pressed her face against his chest as he lifted her from the ground and then again when he staggered up the rocky incline. After that, he was able to stay on a level path, and her crying subsided although it didn't stop.

"This is going to be jarring, Arleta. I'm sorry," he said, when they reached the buggy. She nodded and clung tighter to him, groaning into his chest as he hoisted her into the carriage. After he'd helped her into a sideways sitting position with her leg resting on the seat, he said, "Before we go to the phone shanty to call for help, I need to make a splint to stabilize your ankle. First I have to remove your shoe—"

"*Neh!* Don't touch it!"

"I promise I'll be careful." He gently cupped the sole of her shoe, but she screamed at him to stop. He lifted his head to look into her eyes, but they were squeezed shut as she sobbed. Her complexion was so pale it seemed aglow. "I'm concerned you'll get a worse injury from the carriage jostling around. Please, Arleta, don't make me do that to you. Haven't I caused you enough harm already?"

"I—I—I have a tattoo." She panted the peculiar sentence more than she actually spoke it, and Noah assumed she was delirious with shock. But then she continued, her words coming out in spurts as she cried, "On my ankle. A ta-tattoo of an *Englischer*'s initials inside a heart. I was on *rumspringa*. I was going to leave the Amish. I was going to marry him and I'm—I'm so ashamed..."

And then she passed out.

* * *

Arleta didn't remember any of the buggy ride from the meadow to the phone shanty and little of the ambulance ride from the phone shanty to the hospital. Nor could she recall what the doctor said the name of the second bone was—talus was the first—that she'd broken when she'd slipped into the ditch and landed on the rock. So when the curtains around her gurney in the emergency room parted and Noah peeked inside and gave her a small smile, she wasn't certain whether she was imagining him or not.

But then he came to her side and touched her cheek, just as tenderly as he'd done in the alcove at the pond, and she knew for certain she had to be dreaming, because he never would have looked at her so lovingly in real life—not once she'd told him about her tattoo.

"How do you feel?" he asked, taking his hand away. He wasn't a dream after all.

"A little better. Physically better, anyway. But I'm still so ashamed of…" Now that she wasn't in excruciating pain, Arleta felt too inhibited to repeat that she'd once planned to marry an *Englischer* or that she'd gotten a tattoo. "Of doing those things I told you about."

Noah was quiet a moment before questioning, "Are those things why you don't want to court?"

Lowering her eyes, she nodded.

"Please don't allow something in your past to prevent me from being your suitor now," he implored, his voice quiet but clear as a bell.

Arleta shook her head in disbelief. "How could you want to court me after what I've done?"

"The same way *you* could want to court *me* after what *I've* done."

"It wasn't your fault that your *familye* perished, Noah. *I* sinned deliberately."

He shrugged. "Sin is sin and shame is shame, whether it's big sin or little sin or real shame or false shame... Did you confess your wrongdoings to the Lord?"

"Jah."

"Then He's forgiven you. And as you once told me, you apologized and God has forgiven you so there's no need to continue to feel sorry or to keep apologizing. Otherwise, it's as if you haven't accepted the Lord's forgiveness."

A tear rolled down Arleta's cheek. "But...but how can *you* bear to know I have another *mann's*—an *Englischer's*—initials inscribed on my skin?"

"In my mind, those letters don't stand for another *mann's* name. When I look at them, I see the same thing I see when I look into your eyes. I see that I'm forgiven." Noah repeated slowly, "*I.F.*—I'm. Forgiven. And you're forgiven, too, Arleta. So please, may I be your suitor?"

Arleta fixed her eyes on his. "*Jah*, I'd like that very much," she said.

Epilogue

Noah watched his wife stretch her feet out in front of her. She had eventually confided in her parents about her tattoo and she'd told Sovilla, who'd already had an inkling. And although Arleta knew she was forgiven for her past, Noah had helped pay to have the heart and initials removed, so that it wouldn't become a stumbling block for other people, like Leanna. Now, in late November, Arleta still went barefoot around the house. She said it was to make up for the two years she wore socks every single hour of every single day.

"I can't believe I'm twenty-three, the same age you were when we met," Arleta whispered, rocking their six-month-old daughter to sleep in her arms.

"You're not the same age as I was when I met you—I met you at the *haus* building when I was seventeen."

"*Jah*, that's right," she acknowledged. "What I meant was I can't believe I'm the same age that you were when we started courting. So much has happened in these past three years… Fifteen months of our long-distance courtship. Our wedding. Our *bobbel* being born a year after that. Your *groossmammi*..." She didn't want to finish the thought but Noah finished it for her.

"*Groossmammi* going home to be with the Lord," he said. "You know, she told me once she was ready—but whether *I* was ready or not, her life was in *Gott*'s hands and there was nothing anyone could do to change that."

Arleta chuckled. "That sounds like Sovilla, all right." Just then the baby sighed in her sleep and Noah and Arleta both chuckled.

"*Groossmammi* was so thrilled to see her namesake before she died."

"*Jah*. One day I came into the living room and I caught her telling little Sovilla her secret ingredient for bumbleberry pie. She said it was such a *gut* secret that it was worth sharing, even with a *bobbel*."

"Do you know what else is worth sharing?"

"What?"

Noah crossed the room and sat on the sofa beside his wife. "This," he said, and gave her sweet, gap-toothed mouth a warm kiss.

* * * * *

If you enjoyed this Amish romance from Carrie Lighte, pick up any of the books in her previous miniseries, Amish of Serenity Ridge:

Available now from Love Inspired!

Dear Reader,

Thank you for reading the first book in my new series! I enjoyed using a fictitious town in Maine as the setting of my previous series, Amish of Serenity Ridge, so much that I just had to set my new series, The Amish of New Hope, in Maine, too.

Because I wrote this book when travel was restricted due to the pandemic, I wasn't able to take my annual Maine summer vacation. I missed kayaking, swimming and hiking with my extended family, as well as visiting the local Amish communities for research (and for fudge!). But writing about characters who live in Maine helped me envision the area's lakes, rocky cliffs and pine trees, so at least I got to go there in my mind. I hope you felt transported there, too.

For those of you who bake but have never made a bumbleberry pie like the one Arleta learned to make, I'd encourage you to give it a try. (And if you want to know Sovilla's secret, it's to include a single apple, chopped small, to the berries.) You'll love it and so will your family and friends!

Blessings,
Carrie Lighte

Get 4 FREE REWARDS!

We'll send you 2 FREE Books plus <u>2</u> FREE Mystery Gifts.

Love Inspired books feature uplifting stories where faith helps guide you through life's challenges and discover the promise of a new beginning.

FREE
Value Over
$20